I0758038

Make Love Make Sense
by Raymond A. Raglin III

Introduction

The Language of Love Beyond Words

In the vast spectrum of human experience, love emerges as the most universal yet mysterious emotion, transcending language barriers to touch our essence. It's an intense sentiment that often defies words. While poetry and prose attempt to capture love's journey, its most authentic expressions are felt, tasted, heard, seen, and smelled. This silent language of love conveyed through the senses offers a pathway to understanding affection in its purest form.

Conventional notions of love, confined to verbal and written forms, must acknowledge how emotions are conveyed and received. Consider the solace in a touch or the joy a familiar scent brings, transporting us to love-filled moments. These experiences speak to the heart with a clarity unmatched by words.

Our perceptions aren't just tools for navigating the physical world; they convey intimate aspects of human connection. A lover's gaze, the taste of a shared meal, and the sound of a familiar voice weave the tapestry of love. Each sense offers a unique medium for experiencing and expressing love, crafting an emotional symphony that resonates within.

Through this sensory language, love finds its truest expression. Touch, taste, sound, vision, and smell become the heart's vocabulary, transcending spoken language to enrich the human experience. This unspoken dialogue forms enduring bonds among lovers, family, and friends.

As we delve into the sensory dimensions of love, let's reconsider how it's communicated and felt. Beyond poetry and love letters lies a world of emotional expression awaiting discovery. It's a realm where love isn't just heard but truly listened to, seen but beheld, felt but not spoken. Understanding this language opens us to deeper connections, enriching our lives with unspoken affection and transforming our relationships.

"Make Love Make Sense" isn't just an exploration of love's encounters; it's an invitation to rediscover how we connect, explore love's tranquil language, and express the ineffable. In the following pages, we'll explore each sense's role in our love experiences. Perhaps we'll discover that the most boundless expressions of love elude words entirely.

Objective: Understanding Love Beyond Words

The goal of "Make Love Make Sense" isn't just to explore love's sensory dimensions but to fundamentally shift readers' perspectives on its expression and experience. This book challenges the idea that verbal declarations are love's primary or most significant means of communication. Instead, we propose a broader understanding of love that recognizes consciousness as vital to forming and deepening emotional bonds.

Our aim is twofold: first, to illustrate how our senses enrich our emotional landscapes beyond words; second, to equip readers with insights and tools to cultivate these connections in their relationships.

By broadening our understanding of love beyond words, we emphasize the importance of sensory engagement in emotional bonds. Each chapter will explore one of the five senses—touch, taste, sound, vision, and smell—showcasing how they evoke memories, stir emotions, and strengthen connections in ways language alone cannot. Through narratives, scientific insights, and practical advice, readers will learn to harness the senses' power in relationships.

This exploration doesn't diminish verbal expressions of love but complements them with a broader range of communicative tools. By recognizing sensory engagement's significance, readers can unlock new dimensions of intimacy and understanding, fostering relationships felt, seen, heard, tasted, and smelled.

Ultimately, we aim to inspire a deeper appreciation for love's diverse dimensions, encouraging readers to embrace them in their lives. Through "Make Love Make Sense," we guide readers toward a more nuanced understanding of love that transcends language barriers, fostering richer human connections.

The Five Senses: Gateways to the Heart

In love's realm, our senses are gatekeepers to valuable emotional experiences. They channel love's essence, touching our hearts and souls beyond words. This section delves into each sense—touch, taste, sound, vision, and smell—to enrich our understanding and expression of love. Through this exploration, we aim to lay a conceptual framework that broadens our ability to experience love fully.

Touch: The Language of Comfort and Connection

Touch, primal and pre-verbal, communicates security, warmth, and love. From soothing newborns to comforting embraces, it bridges souls, magnifying empathy and affection in romantic relationships.

Taste: The Flavor of Memories and Moments Shared

Often overlooked, taste evokes memories and forges bonds over shared experiences. A dish can transport us to cherished moments, reigniting emotions associated with first loves and celebrations. Meals become rituals of care, nourishing mind, body, and soul.

Sound: The Harmony of Shared Existence

Sounds—the melody of laughter, the cadence of voices—compose our emotional world. They comfort, energize, and evoke human emotions. Sounds reinforce love's bonds, weaving an auditory melody that underscores our connected lives.

Vision: Seeing and Being Seen

Vision offers the gift of mutual recognition and appreciation. Visual cues—lingering glances, empathetic smiles—communicate love's depth, acknowledging the beauty of souls in their entirety.

Smell: The Scent of Presence and Memory

The most evocative sense, smell, triggers deep emotions and memories. Fragrances anchor us to moments of love, past and present, at once and viscerally.

These senses offer unique paths to experience and express love. As we journey through "Make Love Make Sense," we'll explore each deeply, uncovering how they enrich our relationships and deepen connections. Understanding their contributions invites a fuller, more vibrant emotional life where love is experienced through our essence.

Objective: Beyond Biology—The Senses as Conduits of Love

In exploring love through the five senses, we aim to go beyond their traditional understanding as mere biological functions. We delve into a realm where touch, taste, sound, vision, and smell are acknowledged for their profound significance in connecting with and perceiving love. Our goal is to shed light on how our interactions are intertwined with our emotional lives, shaping and being shaped by the love we give and receive.

Touch: The Embodiment of Connection

Touch becomes a language communicating affection, comfort, and care in ways words cannot. Through touch, we feel love's physical presence, forging bonds at our core. Recognizing touch as a conduit of love allows us to appreciate simple embraces or the gentle touch of hands as acts of connection.

Taste: The Flavor of Intimacy

Taste enriches our love experiences, turning shared meals and flavors into lingering connections. It's how we celebrate traditions, create memories, and find comfort. Viewing taste as a path to emotional connection encourages us to savor togetherness, enriching relationships through sharing.

Sound: The Resonance of Affection

Sounds—voices, laughter, music—carry emotional weight, reinforcing our bonds with others. Sound becomes a medium for expressing and feeling love, from the comfort of a familiar voice to the intimacy of shared silence. Acknowledging sound's emotional power deepens our connections, where love is as much about listening as being heard.

Vision: The Insight of Love

Vision reveals insights into the souls of those we love. Seeing and being seen forms connections based on understanding and recognition. This perspective challenges us to look beyond appearances, finding beauty in the known and felt, cherishing genuine connections visible only to the heart's eye.

Smell: The Essence of Memory and Presence

The sense of smell's direct pathway to our emotions and memories holds unique power in love's landscape. It evokes a person or moment's essence, anchoring us to feelings that transcend time and space. Valuing smell as a vessel for emotional connection acknowledges loved ones' intangible yet powerful presence felt through their scent.

By presenting the five senses as integral to our perceptions of love, we enrich our understanding of love as a multi-sensory experience. This exploration isn't just academic but an odyssey toward a fuller, more embodied love. Through this lens, our senses don't just help us navigate the physical world; they open us to the nuanced spectrum of emotional connection, allowing us to experience love in its most vibrant, tangible forms.

Feeling Love: The Touch that Connects

Touch is a primordial sense, developing first in the human fetus and remaining a crucial means of communication, comfort, and connection throughout our lives. It conveys a range of emotions, from parental protection to romantic passion, speaking volumes without words. This section explores the roles of touch in expressing and experiencing love.

The Comfort of Touch

A gentle hug, a reassuring pat, or a sympathetic touch can provide solace, reduce stress, and display empathy in times of sorrow or uncertainty. The warmth of a comforting embrace offers security and belonging, creating bonds of trust and support essential to emotional well-being.

The Electricity of Intimacy

In romantic relationships, touch is charged with desire and intimacy. From the tentative brush of fingers to a passionate kiss, touch communicates affection and love profoundly. Physical attraction is expressed and intensified, bridging souls and creating a space of vulnerability where love can flourish.

The Language of Non-Verbal Communication

Touch is a nonverbal language that expresses nuanced emotions. A hand touch can convey support, a stroke can offer reassurance, and a nuzzle can express affection. These gestures communicate love in its daily, quiet forms, strengthening relationships.

Touch as a Healing Force

Touch has well-documented healing properties, reducing pain, lowering heart rates, and decreasing anxiety. Within love, touch offers physical and emotional relief, deepening the bond between individuals. It reminds us that love is a force of healing and renewal.

The Universality of Touch

Touch transcends cultural and linguistic barriers, making it a universal expression of love and humanity. It reminds us that we are beings of connection, seeking warmth and comfort from others. Exploring touch as a fundamental expression of love invites us to reconnect with our innate ability for empathy, compassion, and connection.

Recognizing the power of touch to communicate emotions, we open ourselves to infinite love. Embracing touch as a vital part of our emotional lives enriches our relationships and deepens our connections in the most human ways.

Objective: The Influential Power of Touch in Communicating Love

Exploring touch as an essential aspect of expressing and experiencing love underscores its unparalleled role in human connection. The objective is not merely to count how touch manifests within relationships but to highlight its impact on emotional intimacy and psychological well-being. By integrating personal narratives and scientific insights, we emphasize touch's significance, setting the stage for understanding its role in conveying love.

Unveiling the Emotional Depth of Touch

Touch can communicate messages of love and care that transcends language. It bypasses intellectual barriers and communicates directly with our emotional selves. This section unravels the emotional language of touch, from a parent's protective embrace to lovers' intimate caresses. Each gesture is meaningful.

The Science Behind Touch

Scientific insights reveal the physiological and psychological mechanisms activated by touch. Physical contact releases oxytocin, the "love hormone," fostering trust, empathy, and bonding. These findings reinforce touch as an emotional conduit vital for psychological health and developing healthy relationships.

Personal Narratives: The Stories of Touch

Personal narratives powerfully testify to touch's impact. Stories of reunited loved ones, comfort found in a friend's hug during distress, or gentle touches between partners that communicate more than words bring light to how touch manifests in love experiences. These narratives add depth and relatability, showcasing touch's universality as a language of love.

Highlighting the Universality and Nuance of Touch

Touch is a global language transcending cultural and linguistic differences, yet its nuances vary significantly based on context, intention, reception, individual experiences, cultural backgrounds, and personal boundaries. This exploration acknowledges touch's complexity and encourages mindful engagement.

The Healing Power of Touch

Touch's ability to heal, both physically and emotionally, is examined. From therapeutic practices to simple comfort, this aspect underscores the power of human connection through touch to foster healing, resilience, and emotional strength.

By highlighting touch as an influential communicator of love, "Make Love Make Sense" deepens appreciation for relationships' tactile aspects. It encourages harnessing touch's power to express love, enhance emotional connections, and enrich lives with intimacy and understanding.

Tasting Love: The Flavors of Connection

Taste, a sensory pathway to the heart, evokes deep emotions and vivid memories. Like love, taste encompasses a spectrum of flavors—sweet, bitter, sour, and everything in between—each carrying symbolic weight and emotional resonance. This exploration delves into how taste, through meals and culinary traditions, becomes a metaphor for love's complexities, binding people together.

The Sweetness of Shared Moments

Sweetness symbolizes joy and happiness in moments of connection. Shared desserts, birthday cakes, or chocolate tokens of affection transcend immediate pleasure, becoming imbued with lingering memories and emotions. They elucidate love's joyful expressions, weaving a common thread through relationships.

The Bitterness of Growth and Strength

Bitterness reflects challenges and growth opportunities in love. Like the shock of a bitter flavor, encountering relationship difficulties can be unsettling. Yet, as our palate adjusts to appreciate bitter flavors, our emotional understanding deepens through navigating love's challenges. Overcoming adversity, like savoring bitter coffee together, strengthens bonds and enriches relationships.

The Complexity of Flavors and Emotions

A meal's flavor complexity mirrors love's emotional complexity. A well-prepared dish is like a healthy relationship, where different elements create something greater. Cooking for someone is an act of love, a tangible manifestation of care and affection.

Culinary Traditions: The Recipe of Connection

Culinary traditions are vessels for history, culture, and memory, connecting people. Cooking family recipes, exploring a loved one's cuisine, or creating new traditions together bind people across generations and geographies. These experiences become part of a relationship's narrative.

The Emotional Resonance of Taste

Taste transports us to specific moments, evoking emotions and memories. A particular dish can remind us of home, loved ones, and moments of joy, sorrow, and love. This resonance underscores taste's power as an external and emotional experience, connecting us to people, places, and moments that shape us and our understanding of love.

Exploring taste reveals how its complexity, ability to evoke memory, and role in experiences make it a profound metaphor for love. Love, like taste, is multifaceted, evoking a range of emotions and rooted in unique experiences that bind us. Through taste, we savor love's flavors, finding connection, memory, and meaning in meals and culinary traditions that nourish our bodies and hearts.

Objective: Savoring the Essence of Connection Through Taste

The sensory exploration of love brings us to taste, a personal and relatable sense that entwines emotions and cultural identities. This exploration illustrates how taste informs love experiences, bridging gaps between individuals and generations through the language of flavor. Our intent is to delve into the emotional resonance of taste and uncover its cultural significance in human connection. By preparing the reader for stories highlighting taste's role in bonding and memory, we enrich the understanding of love's dimensions.

Unpacking the Emotional Layers of Taste

Taste elicits a spectrum of emotional responses, from comfort to excitement. It evokes memories, transporting us to moments of joy, nostalgia, and melancholy. Personal narratives explore how specific tastes link with cherished memories and relationships, serving as bookmarks in our lives. These stories showcase how taste encapsulates moments of connection, celebration, and loss, highlighting its impact on our emotional world.

Exploring Cultural Traditions Through Flavor

Taste is a gateway to cultural understanding and heritage. Culinary traditions passed down through generations offer a tangible connection to our roots and a way to share histories. This section explores how communion meals and cooking for others can be powerful expressions of love, transcending barriers. Stories delve into the role of taste in cultural identity and intercultural relationships, deepening our view of how flavors foster belonging and connection.

Preparing for a Journey of Sensory Exploration

As we embark on this sensory journey through taste, we engage the reader's palate and heart. The narratives and insights are curated to deepen appreciation for how taste—through its ability to evoke emotion, memory, and cultural connection—plays an integral role in love. This exploration is about understanding the physiological aspects of taste and savoring the emotional and cultural layers that flavor meaningful relationships.

By highlighting taste's significance in love, we invite readers to reflect on culinary memories and traditions, encouraging mindful engagement with flavors that shape emotional and relational worlds. Through love's flavors, we offer a nuanced perspective on how taste contributes to the bonds that define our human experience. We prepare the palate and heart for stories celebrating the link between taste, memory, and love.

Hearing Love: The Soundscapes of Affection

In the rhythm of life, the sounds of love play a melody that resonates within the deepest chambers of our hearts, from a loved one's soothing voice to a favorite song's harmonious chords and laughter's infectious nature. Sound shapes our emotional landscape in incredible ways. This exploration dives into love's auditory expressions, highlighting how sound serves as a backdrop to our experiences and a potent conductor of emotion and connection.

The Voice of Love

Hearing a loved one's voice brings unique comfort—a familiarity and warmth that can calm fears, ignite joy, or make the world feel right. A loved one's voice can be an auditory embrace, wrapping us in safety and belonging. Whether it's a whispered "I love you," the excitement in a greeting after time apart, or gentle consolation during vulnerability, the voice expresses love in all its shades.

Musical Heartstrings

Music, with its universal language, encapsulates emotions, memories, and moments. Songs or melodies become landmarks in our relationships, defining times spent together, feelings experienced, and journeys navigated. Music can transport us back to falling in love, celebrating an anniversary, or grieving a loss, allowing us to relive those emotions anew. Through music, we find a soundtrack to our love stories, each chord and melody enriching our connections' narrative.

Laughter: The Soundtrack of Joy

Contagious laughter weaves through our relationships, creating light-hearted and deeply rooted bonds. Laughter, especially with loved ones, dissolves barriers, heals wounds, and brings us closer. It signifies not just happiness but deep-seated joy from understanding, accepting, and reveling in another's company. In laughter, we find a mutual language of affection, a frequency that resonates with love's vibrancy.

The Silence of Understanding

In sound, silence holds significance in expressing love. The comfortable stillness between individuals speaks to an understanding and connection that transcends words. In quiet moments—the pause to listen, the space to be—a bond's depth can be felt most acutely. A peaceful moment becomes a sound of love, a testament to the comfort and acceptance found in another's presence.

Echoes of Affection

Affection's soundscapes are not merely background noise; they are integral to how we experience and express love. A name called in affection, a lullaby's gentle hum, or a heartbeat's comforting cadence beside us—each is an echo of love, a sonic fingerprint unique to our connections. As we navigate love's complexities, the sounds accompanying our journey become landmarks of affection dedicated to the moments and emotions that define our relationships.

Exploring the sounds we love reminds us how sound enriches our emotional lives. It underscores the importance of listening not just with our ears but with our hearts, attuning ourselves to the melodies of love that play throughout our lives. Through this auditory journey of love, we appreciate how sound—in all its forms—shapes, conveys, and celebrates the profound connections that make life truly resonant.

Objective: The Resonance of Love Through Hearing

The auditory exploration of love aims to unveil the rich emotional landscapes traversed through hearing. This journey through sound is not just about recognizing how love manifests audibly but is committed to illustrating the emotional depth and variety of love's sounds. From a familiar voice's comforting cadence to musical experiences' collective joy, we aim to deepen appreciation for hearing as a powerful vessel for emotional connection and expression of love.

The Comforting Cadence of Familiar Voices

One of the most profound aspects of love we seek to illuminate is the emotional comfort and belonging evoked by a loved one's voice. Whether it's soothing words of reassurance during stress or excited chatter recounting a day's adventure, these voices' familiarity acts as an anchor, grounding us in security and connection. By sharing stories and insights into how voices carry our emotions' weight, we highlight how hearing becomes more than just a sense—it becomes a source of emotional sustenance.

The Shared Harmony of Music

Music's role in expressing and experiencing love transcends cultural and linguistic boundaries to touch hearts universally. Our exploration into music's infectious joy celebrates this universal language of love, showcasing how songs and melodies encapsulate moments, memories, and feelings between people. By examining musical experiences' emotional bonds, we impart the unique joy and communal connection music brings to our lives and relationships.

Laughter: The Universal Melody of Joy

Laughter with loved ones testifies to the moments of pure joy and understanding that define our closest relationships. This exploration delves into laughter's significance as a sonic expression of happiness, affection, and shared experiences. By understanding laughter's role in building and supporting emotional connections, we recognize its importance as a fundamental sound of love, enriching our relationships' emotional chemistry.

The Cryptic Silence of Connection

Recognizing the power of hearing to experience love, we also acknowledge unspoken moments' profound significance. Comfortable silences between loved ones offer a space for unspoken understanding and deep emotional connection. By exploring these moments of quiet communion, we reveal the depth of connection felt without words, highlighting how silence speaks volumes in love's language.

Amplifying the Sounds of Love

We aim to amplify appreciation for how love is heard, felt, and communicated through sound. By conveying love's emotional depth and variety experienced through hearing, we invite readers to attune themselves more closely to the sounds shaping their love stories. Love's sounds surround us, whether in words, music, laughter, or stillness, waiting to be heard with the heart. Through listening to love's languages, we aspire to enrich the reader's understanding of love, celebrating the auditory dimensions that add depth and resonance to our most cherished connections.

Seeing Love: The Visions that Bind

In love's landscape, vision plays a crucial role in shaping perceptions and guiding emotions, from the first flutter of attraction to the profound recognition of a soul mate. This expedition into love's visual aspects explores how sight affects our understanding and experience of love, highlighting how what we see influences what we feel. Through a nuanced discussion, we dive into vision's multilayered role in love, exploring its power to bind individuals in a world of deep understanding.

The Spark of Attraction

The first moment of attraction often begins with a look. This visual connection can ignite the initial spark of interest and desire. Visual cues are complex and influenced by biological instincts, personal preferences, and societal norms. Beyond surface aesthetics, the spark of attraction is also about the potential we see in another—the promise of shared experiences, the glimpse of a kindred spirit, or the recognition of admirable qualities. By exploring initial visual attractions, we delve into the complexity behind "love at first sight," examining how what we see sets the stage for the ensuing emotional journey.

The Gaze of Understanding

As relationships deepen, vision's role shifts from the superficial to the profound. It's no longer just about physical appearance but about seeing and being seen more completely. The gaze between lovers becomes one of understanding and connection, a visual dialogue communicating love, acceptance, and mutual recognition. This gaze transcends verbal communication, carrying empathy, support, and a deep-seated knowledge of the other person. Through stories and reflections, we explore how this deeper sight fosters an emotionally and spiritually fulfilling bond.

The Visibility of Actions

Love is seen not only in the gaze or physical presence but also in actions that manifest feelings and commitments. Acts of care, small gestures of affection, and efforts to bring joy to another's life are all visual expressions of love. These visible actions reinforce emotional bonds, showcasing love as an active, lived experience. By discussing actions' visibility, we highlight how love is not just an emotion felt in the heart but also a series of actions seen and appreciated, further binding individuals together.

The Perspective of Time

Our perspectives on loved ones change as we grow together through shared experiences, struggles, and growth. This changing vision reflects love's dynamic nature, adapting and deepening as we come to appreciate not just the person we initially fell in love with but the person they have become. Time's perspective allows us to see the beauty in the journey, recognizing how love has shaped our perceptions and relationships.

The Clarity of Love's Vision

Exploring love's vision, we adhere to vision's influential role in our love experiences. From the first spark of attraction to the deep understanding that comes with time, what we see profoundly influences how we feel and connect with others. This walk through love's visual dimensions invites us to look beyond the surface, to see not just with our eyes but with our hearts, recognizing the extraordinary ways our visual perceptions bind us to those we love. Through this exploration, we understand that seeing love is about much more than visual attraction—it is about the shared visions that form the foundation of lasting bonds.

Objective: Illuminating the Visual Dimensions of Love

Love's exploration through vision's lens sets out to unravel the intricate dance between visual cues and the deep, emotional currents of attraction and connection. Our aim transcends the surface-level understanding of visual appeal, delving into how truly seeing someone—aesthetically, emotionally, and spiritually—constitutes a fundamental aspect of love. This exploration aims to shed light on vision's layered role in igniting love's spark and nurturing its growth over time.

Beyond the Surface: The Initial Spark

Our journey through love's visual dimensions acknowledges physical attraction's undeniable role, recognizing it as a natural and powerful force in the genesis of romantic relationships. However, our exploration probes deeper, examining how visual cues—gestures, expressions, and actions—serve as the first alphabet in love's language. By weaving together insights from psychology, art, and personal narratives, we illustrate how these early visual impressions can signify more than physical appeal, hinting at personality traits, emotional availability, and potential for deeper connection.

The Gaze of Connection: Seeing and Being Seen

Central to our exploration is the gaze's transformative power in establishing and deepening emotional connections. This section touches on the psychology of eye contact, exploring how looking into someone's eyes can foster feelings of vulnerability, intimacy, and mutual understanding. Through stories that capture moments of connection strengthened by a shared gaze, we highlight how genuinely seeing someone—and allowing oneself to be seen—embodies the essence of emotional closeness and trust in love.

Visual Expressions of Love: Actions and Symbols

Expanding our inquiry's scope, we examine how love manifests in visual expressions beyond the gaze—through actions, symbols, and shared experiences. This includes body language's nuanced communication, gifts and tokens of affection's symbolic value, and the loving creation of visual memories that become landmarks in a relationship's journey. By exploring how these visual expressions contribute to a relationship's essence, we underscore the importance of sight not just in attraction but in continuously nurturing and affirming love.

The Evolution of Sight: Deepening Perception Over Time

Recognizing love as a dynamic journey, our exploration considers how visual perception evolves within a lasting relationship's context. As love matures, the way we see our partners often shifts, reflecting a deeper understanding and appreciation for their complexities, strengths, and vulnerabilities. This section aims to celebrate the beauty of this evolving vision, illustrating how love's depth is mirrored in the depth of our seeing—beyond physical appearances to the essence of the person we love.

A Deep Aspect of Seeing Love

In concluding our exploration, we reaffirm vision's significance in love—not merely as sensory input but as a deeper aspect of human connection. By exploring visual cues' role in attraction and the profound implications of truly seeing someone, we invite readers to reflect on their own experiences of love and vision. Through love's enduring journey through the heart's eyes, we aim to enrich the understanding of how seeing, in all its forms, is integral to how we encounter, express, and grow in love. Our goal is not just to illuminate love's visual dimensions but to inspire a greater appreciation for the visual cues that connect us, the gaze's transformative power, and the profound act of genuinely seeing someone as an expression of deep, enduring love.

Smelling Love: The Scent of Memory

In the intricate weave of human experience, scent holds a unique and profound place, particularly in love and memory. It's an invisible thread in the complex web of our lives, capable of instantly transporting us across time and space to moments steeped in emotion. This exploration into the powerful link between scent and memory delves into how fragrances—whether a person's natural scent, a meal's aroma, or a momentous day's particular perfume—become inextricably tied to our love and connection.

The Essence of Presence

At the heart of scent's power is its ability to evoke a person's essence. The subtle blend of perfume or cologne, the natural scent of skin, or the comforting smell of home cooking can instantly bring a loved one's presence to mind, evoking a flood of emotions and memories. This section explores how these personal scents become deeply embedded in our memories, serving as olfactory snapshots that keep our connections to loved ones alive, even in their absence.

The Fragrance of Spaces and Moments

Spaces and experiences often carry distinct scents that, over time, become markers of moments spent with loved ones. The smell of a particular spice in the air, the fresh scent of nature during an outdoor adventure, or the comforting aroma of a familiar home can all trigger vivid recollections of times of togetherness and love. Through personal stories and scientific insights, we examine how these shared scents solidify our memories of moments and enrich our emotional landscape.

Scent as a Bridge to the Past

Scent's unique ability to bypass the conscious mind and directly trigger emotional memories makes it a powerful bridge to the past. A sudden whiff of a long-forgotten fragrance can resurrect feelings of love and nostalgia, sharply bringing past affection, joy, or even loss into the present. This section explores the neuroscience behind this phenomenon, investigating how scent and memory are entwined in the brain and how this connection reinforces love's enduring power.

The Role of Scent in Emotional Healing and Connection

Beyond its ability to evoke memories, scent also plays a role in emotional healing and connection. A loved one's comforting smell can provide solace during stress or grief as a sensory affirmation of support and love. Additionally, sharing scents—through the gift of perfume, the exchange of clothing, or the creation of an olfactory environment—can deepen bonds and foster a sense of belonging. This exploration considers how scent can be consciously used to nurture relationships and support emotional well-being.

The Lingering Fragrance of Love

As we journey through the olfactory landscape of love, we reflect on scent's lingering impact on our perceptions of love and memory. The fragrances associated with our most cherished moments and people continue to resonate within us, evoking emotions and memories that define our love. By understanding the deep connection between scent and memory, we gain insight into the invisible yet indelible ways love permeates our lives, leaving a lasting fragrance that continues to shape our hearts and memories.

In delving into love's subtle scent, we not only celebrate the scent's evocative power in recalling past loves and moments of connection but also recognize its role in the ongoing narrative of our emotional lives. Through this exploration, we come to appreciate the subtle yet profound ways in which the scents we encounter become integral to our experience of love, binding us to our past, enriching our present, and continuing to influence our future connections.

Objective: Unraveling the Essence of Scent in Love and Memory

This thought-provoking journey through love's intangible fragrance aims to unravel and illuminate the intricate relationship between scent, memory, and emotion. This exploration seeks to dig deep into how scent acts not just as a passive backdrop to our lives but as a dynamic, evocative force capable of triggering profound emotional responses and vivid recollections of moments filled with love and intimacy. Through a blend of scientific insights, personal narratives, and reflective analysis, we aim to elucidate how scents are woven into the fabric of our emotional and relational experiences.

The Science of Scent and Memory

Central to our exploration is the scientific foundation that explains why scent has such a potent connection to memory and emotion. The olfactory system's direct link to the limbic system, the brain's emotional center, means that scents bypass the more analytical parts of the brain and evoke feelings and memories in an immediate, unfiltered manner. By unpacking the neuroscience behind this phenomenon, we aim to provide readers with a deeper understanding of how and why certain smells can powerfully evoke the past and the emotions tied to those memories, including those of love and intimacy.

Personal Narratives: The Stories Scents Tell

To illustrate scent's impact on our emotional lives, we will share personal stories highlighting how specific fragrances have triggered memories of significant others, cherished moments, and deep emotional connections. These narratives serve as vivid examples of scent's power to transport us back to moments of love—whether it's the perfume worn on a first date, the smell of a grandparent's home, or the distinct aroma of a holiday meal. Through these stories, readers will see scent's universal yet profoundly personal role in our lives, acting as a key to unlocking memories and emotions long stored away.

Emotional Landscapes Shaped by Scent

Further, we delve into the emotional landscapes shaped by our olfactory senses. Scent not only recalls memories but also evokes nostalgia, longing, comfort, and love. This section explores how certain scents become imbued with emotional significance, coloring our perceptions of past relationships and moments of intimacy. We aim to show how scent can be a source of joy, reminding us of loved ones and happy times, as well as a catalyst for melancholy, bringing to mind what we have lost or left behind.

The Role of Scent in Creating and Maintaining Bonds

Lastly, we examine how scent plays an active role in creating and nurturing emotional bonds. From the deliberate choice of perfume to remind a partner of oneself to the creation of scented memories, such as cooking together or exploring nature, scent becomes a medium through which relationships are nurtured and sustained. This section underscores scent's potential to not only trigger memories of love and intimacy but also contribute to a relationship's ongoing story.

The Enduring Fragrance of Memory and Emotion

In concluding our exploration, we reaffirm scent's unique position at the intersection of memory and emotion, serving as a powerful, evocative trigger for recalling the depths of love and intimacy experienced throughout our lives.

By understanding how intricately scent is intertwined with our most cherished memories and emotions, we gain insight into its enduring impact on our hearts and minds. Through love's essence, we invite readers to rediscover and celebrate the scents that have shaped their love stories, recognizing them as invaluable keys to the treasure trove of their emotional past.

Sensory Love: A World Woven Together

As we draw our exploration to a close, we find ourselves enveloped in a rich tapestry of sensory love, a complex and vibrant weave of touch, taste, sound, vision, and scent. Each sense, a unique strand in the fabric of our emotional lives, contributes hues and textures to how we experience and understand love. This concluding section synthesizes these sensory threads, highlighting their collective role in shaping our perceptions of love and the essence of how we connect, share, and thrive within its embrace.

The Harmony of the Senses

Our journey through the senses reveals that love, in its most profound form, transcends language's limitations. It is in the harmony of touch, taste, sound, vision, and scent that love finds its fullest expression. This multisensory engagement allows us to experience love's depth and breadth in a profoundly personal and universally understood way. The gentle caress of a loved one, the flavors of a meal, the resonance of a familiar voice, the sight of a smile, and the scent that recalls a cherished moment—each encounter enriches our understanding of love, adding layers of meaning and connection.

Interweaving Sensory Memories and Emotions

The memories and emotions woven into our senses further embellish love's tapestry. Each sense is a gateway to the past, evoking vivid memories and the emotions tied to them. These memories form the backdrop against which our current love experiences are framed, informing our connections and guiding our interactions. By recognizing each sense's role in recalling and creating memories, we appreciate how the senses serve as milestones in our emotional journey, marking the path of our relationships.

The Dynamic Nature of Sensory Love

As we navigate life, how we engage with and perceive love through our senses evolves. New experiences add layers to its texture, changing its pattern. This dynamic nature reflects the growth and transformation inherent in love. By staying open to the many ways love can be sensed, we allow our understanding and expression of love to mature, deepening our connections and enriching our lives.

Embracing the Full Spectrum of Love

To truly understand and appreciate love in all its complexity, we are called to engage with it through all our senses. This multisensory approach invites a more holistic understanding that embraces the full spectrum of emotions, from the heights of joy to the depths of sorrow. It encourages us to be present, to savor each moment, and to find beauty in the myriad ways love touches our lives.

The Essence of Sensory Love

In concluding our exploration, we reaffirm the central thesis of our journey: that love's essence is best understood and experienced through a symphony of sensory engagement. The tapestry of love, woven from the strands of touch, taste, sound, vision, and scent, offers a more nuanced and vibrant understanding that celebrates its complexity and cherishes its depth. As we move forward, let us carry an appreciation for love's sensory dimensions, allowing them to guide us in deepening our connections and enriching our lives with the subtle beauty of love in all its forms.

Objective: Weaving Together the Sensory Strands of Love

Our aim is precise and multifaceted as we stand at the threshold of this immersive exploration into love's sensory dimensions. We aim to synthesize the insights gathered, weaving them into a cohesive understanding that positions love as an experience far beyond verbal expression. This journey is not merely about acknowledging love's sensory aspects but about deeply engaging with them and recognizing how they collectively shape our perceptions, emotions, and connections. Through this synthesis, we seek to reinforce the concept of love as a rich, multi-sensory experience, setting a tone of discovery and reflection for the exploration to come.

Beyond Words: The Essence of Sensory Engagement

At our exploration's heart is the recognition that love transcends language's limitations in its most authentic forms. Though powerful, words are but one medium through which love is expressed and understood. We aim to illuminate the depth and breadth of love conveyed through touch, taste, sound, vision, and scent—each sense opening a unique pathway to the heart and soul of human connection. By delving into these sensory experiences, we invite readers to expand their understanding of love, embracing it as a dynamic and multifaceted phenomenon that engages all aspects of our being.

The Incalculable Sensory Memories and Emotions

Integral to our intention is exploring how senses are interwoven with memories and emotions, creating a vibrant and intricate web of loving connections. Each sensory encounter with love adds a thread to this tapestry, enriching our emotional landscape and deepening our connections. We aim to showcase how these memories evoke past moments of love and serve as a foundation for ongoing and future relationships, continually shaping our understanding of love.

Setting the Tone for Discovery

As we embark on this exploration, we aim to set a tone of discovery, curiosity, and reflection. We encourage readers to approach this journey with an open heart and mind, ready to explore how love touches our lives through the senses. This exploration is an invitation to rediscover love in its various forms, to appreciate the subtle nuances that each sense brings to our experiences, and to find new depths of connection in our relationships.

Embracing the Multi-Sensory Experience of Love

By reinforcing the concept of love as a rich, multi-sensory experience, we aim to leave readers with a deeper appreciation for the complex and beautiful ways love manifests in our lives. By synthesizing the insights presented, we strive to inspire a more holistic engagement with love that acknowledges the power of the senses in shaping our perceptions, emotions, and connections. As we move forward into the immersive exploration of each sense, let us carry the understanding that to truly know love, we must engage with it through all the senses.

By allowing ourselves to be fully immersed in the sensory symphony that binds us together, we can genuinely appreciate love's multi-sensory nature.

Touch: The Comfort of Connection

The Story of Maya and Her Father

Maya's heart races with excitement and nervousness as she enters the bustling arrivals hall. She scans the crowd and spots her father, a figure of unwavering love and patience, amidst the sea of faces. The years apart have grayed his hair, but his warm, inviting nature remains unchanged. Maya quickens her pace, her luggage trailing behind her.

Their embrace is a world unto itself—a sanctuary of warmth in the impersonal airport. Maya closes her eyes, breathing in the familiar scent of home emanating from her father. His firm, secure arms around her dissolve the weight of years and distance. No words are needed; the touch conveys all the love, relief, and happiness that words might struggle to capture.

This hug and the silent conversation between father and daughter speak volumes. It reassures the constancy of family love, a physical manifestation of the saying, "No matter how far you go, you can always come home." For Maya, feeling her father's steady heartbeat against hers reminds her of her family's foundational role in her life, a touchstone to which she can always return.

As they step back, still holding each other at arm's length, Maya's father looks into her eyes—a gaze filled with pride and joy. His touch shifts to a gentle hold of her shoulders, a gesture that says, "I see you. I acknowledge the person you've become." It's a touch that bridges the gap time has created, reaffirming their bond and the unspoken commitment to support and love each other, regardless of distance or time apart.

The path home is filled with conversation and laughter, but the silent moments, too, are comfortable, punctuated only by the occasional squeeze of Maya's hand or pat on the back—each touch a reaffirmation of their connection. As Maya falls asleep in her childhood room that night, the day's events replay in her mind. It's the hug at the airport, the intensity of touch, that lingers longest, encapsulating the essence of her return—the comfort of connection, the warmth of unconditional love, and the grounding presence of family.

Poetic Perspective:

In the heart of arrivals, a hall bustling and wide,
Maya steps through the threshold, heart swelling with tide.
Amongst the sea of strangers, a familiar form does stand,
Her father a beacon of patience, a guiding, loving hand.

Years have spun their stories in silver threads and grace,
Yet his warmth remains unchanging in this vast, impersonal space.
With hurried steps, she crosses the divide,
Her luggage forgotten in the reunion's eager stride.

Their embrace, a sanctuary found,
In the cacophony of life's surround.
Eyes closed, she breathes in deep,
The scent of home, her heart to keep.

In his arms, a world apart,
Years and distance fade to art.
No words spoken, yet much is said,
In the silence, their love is read.

A conversation, silent and deep,
Promises made, promises to keep.
"You can always come home," the unspoken creed,
In this embrace, their bond is freed.

As they part, still in love's hold,
His gaze upon her, proud and bold.
A gentle touch, a silent speech,
A gap of time, their love does breach.

Homebound, their journey marked by laughter's song,
And silent moments where hearts belong.
The night brings dreams, memories to keep,
Of the hug that lingers, even in sleep.

A touch, a hug, where love is found,
In the quiet, where life's truths abound.
The essence of return, of bonds that tie,
In the comfort of family, under the vast sky.

This is the story, in verses spun,
Of Maya and her father, united as one.
A tale of love's quiet power, so profound,
In the taste of home, where true peace is found.

Reflection

Maya and her father's narrative revolves around the powerful simplicity of a hug, reminding us of touch's vital role in expressing and reaffirming love. In our lives, filled with words spoken and unspoken, it's often the tactile moments that we carry with us—the ones that shape our memories and define our relationships. Through the language of touch, we communicate the depths of our love, finding comfort and connection in its embrace. Maya and her father's story encapsulates touch's emotional resonance as a conduit for expressing and reinforcing familial bonds, underscoring its irreplaceable role in human connection. The detailed portrayal of their airport reunion discusses several key themes and insights into the nature of love, family, and the nonverbal communication that touch embodies:

The Universality of Touch

The narrative highlights touch as a universal language of love and connection, transcending cultural, linguistic, and individual differences. Maya's embrace of her father exemplifies how physical contact can communicate complex emotions such as joy, love, and relief more eloquently than words.

Emotional Connectivity and Reassurance

The story shows how touch is an emotional anchor, offering comfort and reassurance. Maya's father's embrace is a physical manifestation of safety and belonging, signaling that the emotional bond remains unbroken despite the distance and time apart.

The Healing Power of Touch

Maya's reception at the airport, characterized by the warmth and security of her father's hug, illustrates touch's inherent ability to heal and soothe. In moments of reunion or reconciliation, touch can function as a powerful agent of emotional healing, bridging gaps created by absence or misunderstanding.

Touch as a Reflection of Time and Change

The narrative subtly conveys the passage of time and its impact on relationships through touch. Maya notices her father's changes, the physical markers of time's passage, through their embrace. Yet, the familiarity and comfort found in touch affirm that some aspects of love and connection remain constant, unaffected by time.

Nonverbal Communication and Understanding

The story underlines the significant role of nonverbal cues in understanding and empathy. Maya and her father's physical closeness and touch allow for a deep, wordless exchange of emotions, showcasing how touch can convey understanding, acceptance, and mutual recognition in ways that words cannot.

Memory and Sensory Experience

Maya's embrace with her father is depicted as a sensory moment she treasures. This highlights how touch is immediate in its impact and lasting in the memories it creates. Such moments become touchstones in our lives, evoking love and connection long after the moment has passed.

Foundational Importance of Family Bonds

The simplicity and profundity of a hug reiterate the fundamental importance of family bonds. It's evidence of the enduring nature of familial love, a reminder that no matter the distance or time apart, family remains a source of unconditional support and love.

The vibrant recounting of Maya's reunion with her father invites readers to reflect on touch's essential role in their lives. It serves as a poignant reminder of the depth and complexity of love shown through simple, tactile moments, urging an appreciation for the nonverbal expressions of affection that enrich our relationships and emotional landscapes.

Michael and Clara's Language of Silent Support

Michael and Clara lived in a quiet suburb of a busy city. Their love was punctuated by life's trials and triumphs. Their journey together had woven a rich tapestry of shared experiences. Yet, their bond found its most subtle expression in the moments of unspoken support communicated through touch.

Clara, a dedicated teacher, had recently embarked on the challenging quest of earning her master's degree while balancing her professional responsibilities. Michael, her steadfast partner, watched as stress and exhaustion began to etch themselves into Clara's once vibrant demeanor.

One evening, Michael quietly entered the room as Clara sat hunched over a mound of research papers and textbooks, the weight of her aspirations pressing down upon her. Without a word, he knelt beside her chair, gently placing his hands on her weary shoulders. This simple act of touch—a subtle message of understanding and empathy—spoke volumes. Clara's tense muscles relaxed under his hands, a sigh escaping her lips as she leaned back into his comforting presence.

Michael's hands moved with care, easing the knots of tension with each stroke, a quiet testament to his unwavering support. In this delicate exchange, no words were needed; Michael's touch conveyed everything Clara needed to hear: "I'm here for you, I believe in you, and I love you."

Their ritual of touch became a sanctuary of support and love. Each touch strengthened their bond, whether it was a gentle hand squeeze before Clara's important presentation or a comforting arm around her after a long day. It provided solace and comfort, eliminating the need for words.

As months passed, Clara's hard work bore fruit, her efforts culminating in completing her degree. The night of her graduation, amidst the celebration and congratulations, Clara sought out Michael's eyes across the room. Their gaze met, a seamless conversation flowing between them, full of gratitude and love. Later, as they stood alone under the starlit sky, Clara wrapped her arms around Michael in a heartfelt embrace. This time, it was her turn to offer gratitude and love—a touch that said, "Thank you for being my rock, my comfort, and my strength."

Poetic Perspective:

In the quiet suburb's embrace, beneath the city's ceaseless hum,
Michael and Clara's love, through silent support, did come.
A journey shared, of trials and triumphs, side by side,
Their strongest bond in silent moments did reside.

Clara, with dreams of academia's challenging quest,
Found in Michael, a partner, her constant and her best.
Stress etched lines upon her brow, once light and free,
Until Michael's touch whispered, "Lean awhile on me."

One evening, as papers sprawled like leaves in autumn's gust,
Michael entered, his approach silent, his intent just.
Beside her, he knelt, his hands on shoulders laid,
A touch conveying solace as her tensions began to fade

With each gentle stroke, a language of care was spoken,
In the warmth of his hands, her worries were broken.
No words passed between, yet everything was said,
In the language of touch, their love was fed.

This ritual of comfort, of hands offering peace,
Became their haven, where all anxieties would cease.
A squeeze of the hand, an arm's embrace at day's end,
In these gestures, love and support did blend.

Months passed, and Clara's toil turned to triumph bright,
Her dreams achieved, on graduation's celebrated night.
Across a room of cheers, their eyes did meet,
In that glance, a silent dialogue, tender and sweet.

Beneath the stars, in the quiet night's air,
Clara's embrace spoke of gratitude rare.
"Thank you," her touch said, "for being my guide,
My rock, my comfort, where my fears could confide."

Thus, in the realm of unspoken care,
Michael and Clara's love grew ever more fair.
Through the language of touch, their connection did thrive,
In each silent support, their love found its drive.

In this tale of subtlety, of silent bonds that sing,
We find love's quiet strength, in the support it can bring.
A testament to the power of touch, to comfort and to mend,
Michael and Clara's story, where silent support lends.

Reflection

Michael and Clara's story eloquently conveys the power of touch in communicating love and support within a partnership. It highlights how, even without words, simple gestures of affection and understanding can provide deep solace and strength. Through their relationship, we see how touch is a physical expression of love and a vital language of mutual support, binding partners together in the face of life's challenges. Michael and Clara's tale showcases the profound yet often understated power of touch as a medium of communication, support, and connection in intimate relationships. This narrative serves multiple purposes, each enriching the reader's understanding of love's complexities and depth as experienced through touch.

Communicating Support Without Words

The central theme is touch's ability to express deep emotional support and understanding without verbal communication. Michael's actions—his gentle touch and the comfort he provides Clara during her moments of stress and exhaustion—demonstrate how physical expressions of love can speak louder than words. This aspect highlights touch's intuitive and empathetic nature in relationships, where partners can sense and respond to each other's needs in a deeply personal and meaningful way.

The Strengthening of Bonds Through Shared Struggles

Michael and Clara portray how struggles and mutual support strengthen relational bonds. Michael's physical presence and comfort through touch become integral to Clara's journey, symbolizing their partnership's resilience and their reciprocal pact of support. This narrative illustrates the challenges couples face together and how their nonverbal support can deepen their connection and enhance their appreciation for one another.

Touch as a Symbol of Unwavering Presence

The story explores the theme of unwavering presence in a relationship through the lens of touch. Michael's consistent physical support for Clara—through comforting touches or celebratory embraces—is a tangible manifestation of his commitment and love. It reassures Clara of his constant presence and unwavering support, reinforcing the security and trust foundational to their relationship.

Emotional Healing and Relief Through Physical Connection

The narrative reveals touch's healing aspects, showing how physical connection can provide emotional relief and comfort. Clara's physical relaxation in response to Michael's touch underscores physical contact's stress-relieving and soothing power. This aspect invites readers to consider touch's therapeutic potential within their relationships, emphasizing its role in emotional well-being and stress alleviation.

Mutual Gratitude and Recognition

The story culminates in a moment of mutual gratitude and recognition as Clara reciprocates Michael's support with an embrace of her own. This exchange symbolizes the balance of giving and receiving in a relationship, showcasing how gestures of touch offer support and acknowledge and appreciate one's partner's love and effort. It highlights love's reciprocal nature and the importance of recognizing and valuing each other's contributions to the relationship.

Through its exploration of touch, Michael and Clara's story conveys how the sense of touch enriches and deepens love. It emphasizes that touch, in its various forms, is not merely a physical interaction but a profound language of love, offering comfort, support, and connection without the need for words. Through this narrative, readers are invited to reflect on the quiet yet powerful conversations of love that unfold through touch, recognizing its significance in the tapestry of human relationships.

Lucas and Emma's Journey Through Touch

Lucas and Emma navigate the early stages of their relationship and discover touch's complex language, a sensory dialogue that guides them deeper into intimate connection. Their path, marked by the exploration of touch, is a remarkable communication that lays the foundation for love and understanding.

Their story begins with a hesitant yet electrifying first contact—a tentative brush of fingers over a coffee cup. This fleeting moment of touch ignites a spark, an acknowledgment of mutual interest that words could not convey as effectively. Lucas and Emma navigate this new terrain, where every touch is a word in their unfolding dialogue, speaking volumes of curiosity, attraction, and the desire to connect more deeply.

As their relationship deepens, Lucas becomes attuned to Emma's moments of stress and uncertainty, often manifest in the furrow of her brow or the tense set of her shoulders. He learns the language of comfort through touch, offering gentle back rubs or a reassuring hand caress. These gestures become their sanctuary, a tangible reassurance of presence and support. Emma, in turn, reciprocates with her own vocabulary of touch, resting her head on Lucas's shoulder, conveying trust and the comfort of a loving presence.

The path of love is not without its challenges, and for Lucas and Emma, touch often bridges their moments of misunderstanding or distance. A simple hug after a disagreement becomes their olive branch, an unspoken apology, and a promise of reconciliation. In these moments, touch's power as a healing force shines, showing its capacity to soothe emotional wounds and reaffirm their bond.

With time, Lucas and Emma's touches evolve into a language rich with personal meaning—a caress that says, "I'm here for you," a nuzzle that whispers, "I understand," a handhold that shouts, "I love you." This intricate language of touch becomes the bedrock of their connection, offering a way to express their deepest feelings and desires. In quiet moments, illuminated by the soft glow of the bedside lamp, they whisper their most intimate conversations without uttering a single word.

Through Lucas and Emma's journey, we remember touch's innate power to communicate, comfort, and connect. It reiterates that touch, in all its forms, is not just a physical act but a boundless expression of human emotion and connection. It underscores the importance of rediscovering this universal language and encourages us to embrace touch as a vital part of romantic relationships and as a fundamental human need for empathy, connection, and love.

Poetic Perspective:

In early days of whispers soft and light,
Lucas and Emma stepped into love's sight.
A brush of fingers, a moment caught,
In the language of touch, a dialogue sought.

A spark ignited, no words could say,
The volumes spoken in their tactile play.
Each touch, a word in their silent exchange,
A story of love, vast and strange.

Lucas, attuned to Emma's unspoken fears,
Learned to comfort, to soothe her tears.
With a gentle caress, a language they found,
In the sanctuary of touch, their hearts were bound.

Emma, in turn, her affection did show,
With a rest on a shoulder, letting her trust grow.
Their vocabulary of touch, rich and deep,
In the embrace of love, promises they must keep.

Challenges met, with touch they faced,
In a hug, an apology, their misunderstandings erased.
The healing power of touch, a force so bright,
Mending their bond, making it right.

Over time, their touches spoke of more,
A caress, a nuzzle, emotions in store.
"I'm here," "I understand," "I love you,"
In the language of touch, their connection true.

In the quiet glow of night's embrace,
Their love found expression in the simplest space.
Without words, their hearts did speak,
In the language of touch, love at its peak.

Through Lucas and Emma's journey of feel,
The power of touch, to heal, to reveal.
A reminder of the depth of human connection,
In the simple act of touch, love's reflection.

This tale of touch, in whispers and sighs,
Testimonial to love, under open skies.
In every caress, every embrace so sweet,
The language of touch, where hearts meet.

Reflection

Lucas and Emma's narrative, woven through the language of touch, portrays how this essential sense becomes a guiding light in their love story. It highlights touch's role in building and sustaining emotional intimacy and showcases its unmatched ability to convey love's complexities and nuances. Through their journey, we are invited to reflect on our own touch experiences and recognize their transformative power in deepening our connections and enriching our lives with a profound sense of understanding and affection. Lucas and Emma evocatively explore touch as an essential element of emotional intimacy and communication within romantic relationships. This narrative dives into how touch works as a language, capable of expressing complex emotions and forging deep connections without words. Through their story, it portrays critical aspects of how touch influences and enriches love:

Touch as the Foundation of Connection

Lucas and Emma's evolving use of touch mirrors their deepening relationship, from tentative contact to more assured expressions of support and comfort. This progression illustrates how touch, even in its simplest forms, lays the groundwork for building trust, fostering mutual interest, and establishing a unique, unspoken dialogue between partners. It emphasizes that touch is not merely supplementary to verbal communication but foundational to forming and strengthening emotional bonds.

Nonverbal Communication and Emotional Expression

The narrative highlights touch as a powerful nonverbal communication that transcends language's limitations in expressing emotions. Through Lucas and Emma's interactions, we see how touch conveys comfort, love, reassurance, apology, and understanding—often more eloquently than words. This aspect showcases the intrinsic human ability to communicate complex emotional states through physical contact, enriching a relationship's emotional depth and understanding.

The Healing Power of Touch

By depicting moments where touch serves as a means to soothe, heal, and reconcile after misunderstandings or conflicts, the story reflects on touch's ability to mend emotional rifts and reaffirm unity and commitment. This healing aspect underscores touch's role in supporting a relationship's resilience and navigating and overcoming its inevitable challenges, highlighting how physical closeness can function as a powerful catalyst for emotional recovery and reassurance.

Intimacy Through Personalized Touch

As their relationship matures, Lucas and Emma develop a personalized language of touch, with specific gestures laden with unique significance and meaning. This evolution reflects their deepening intimacy, where touch reflects their individual and shared experiences, desires, and understandings. It portrays how, within long-term relationships, touch evolves into an intimate dialogue that continually reaffirms and deepens the connection between partners.

Rediscovery and Reaffirmation of Touch's Universal Importance

Finally, the story invites readers to reconsider and reaffirm touch's value in their lives and relationships. By weaving through touch's various dimensions in emotional connection, the narrative reminds us of the universal need for physical closeness and its immeasurable impact on our emotional well-being and the quality of our relationships.

Through its detailed and sensitive portrayal of touch, Lucas and Emma's story offers a nuanced understanding of how this sense becomes integral to the emotional and communicative fabric of romantic relationships. It encourages readers to reflect on touch's subtle yet expressive power in conveying love, navigating life's challenges together, and enriching the depth of intimacy and partnership.

Taste: The Flavor of Heritage and Togetherness

Elena and Marco's Culinary Odyssey

Elena, whose roots are deeply embedded in Sicily's rich soils, and Marco, whose heritage dances to Salvador's vibrant rhythms, embarked on a journey not just of the heart but of taste. Their love story, seasoned with the flavors of their diverse backgrounds, testified to culinary exploration's power in bridging worlds and blending cultures.

Their voyage began in their first apartment's modest kitchen, where garlic and olive oil's aroma mingled with lime and cilantro's zest. Here, amid pots and pans, they introduced each other to recipes passed down through generations. Elena's hands, deft and assured, crafted the perfect Sicilian Caponata, its sweet and sour essence enveloping the space. With equal enthusiasm, Marco responded with pupusas, their savory filling a homage to his Salvadoran roots. Each meal was a revelation, a sensory immersion into their families' history and heart. This exploration through taste became their ritual, a sacred time to honor and learn about the lineage that coursed through their veins.

As their repertoire expanded, so did their desire to experiment. The kitchen became their laboratory, a place of fearless culinary ventures where boundaries blurred, and new flavors emerged. Here, the Sicilian Arancini met the Salvadoran Beans, a daring yet harmonious fusion symbolizing their entwined lives. These culinary experiments, while sometimes successful, were always meaningful. With each meal, Elena and Marco wove a new strand into their shared identity, a blend distinctly theirs.

Over time, their culinary adventures took on a new dimension as they began creating unique traditions for their union. The annual "Fusion Feast," celebrating the anniversary of their first meal cooked together, became a cherished tradition. Friends and family were invited to partake in a banquet celebrating the melding of Sicilian and Salvadoran cuisines and the beauty of cultural unity and love. It was evident in their belief that love, like cooking, thrives on experimentation, patience, and the willingness to blend different elements into something uniquely beautiful.

Years into their journey, the kitchen bore the marks of their culinary adventures: a collection of spices from around the world, well-worn recipe books annotated with notes, and photographs capturing moments of laughter and culinary triumph. Elena and Marco, now parents, watched with tender eyes as their children navigated this same kitchen, curious hands reaching for the dough, eager to be part of this legacy of love and flavor.

Their narrative, rich with the tastes of heritage and togetherness, powerfully reminds us that sharing meals transcends mere nourishment. It is a communion, a celebration of the flavors that define us and those that unite us. By blending Sicilian and Salvadoran cuisines, Elena and Marco discovered each other's roots and their own. They crafted a future filled with the promise of new traditions, tastes, and the enduring power of love.

Poetic Perspective:

In a kitchen where Sicily's soil meets Salvador's dance,
Elena and Marco start their culinary romance.
Garlic, olive oil, lime, and cilantro blend,
A journey of flavors, where cultures extend.

Elena, with Caponata, sweet and sour,
Crafts dishes with love, hour by hour.
Marco responds, with pupusas in hand,
A taste of his land, so grand.

Each meal, a revelation, a history unfurled,
A sensory journey through a culinary world.
Their ritual of taste, a sacred endeavor,
To honor their heritage, forever and ever.

As dishes mingle, boundaries blur,
Arancini meets beans, aromas stir.
A fusion of flavors, so bold and new,
A journey of a love that grew.

With time, traditions they start to weave,
A "Fusion Feast" on their sleeves.
Family and friends, around the table they gather,
Celebrating love, in culinary lather.

The kitchen, marked by adventure and spice,
Becomes a legacy of love, so nice.
Children reach for dough, eager to partake,
In a story of love, and the meals we make.

Elena and Marco, through taste, they teach,
That love is a flavor within our reach.
By blending their worlds, so rich and deep,
They sow a future, theirs to keep.

This tale of flavors, so vivid and true,
Shows how taste can guide us through.
In meals shared, and traditions born,
Love finds its taste, in the heart of the morn.

Reflection

Through their culinary journey, Elena and Marco illustrate that taste is not just a sensory experience but a vessel for exploring and expressing love. Their story invites us to consider how food—its preparation, sharing, and enjoyment—can be a powerful medium for connecting with others, honoring our heritage, and creating new legacies of togetherness. Elena and Marco's culinary adventure is a rich tapestry combining compelling themes and lessons about love, culture, and connection. Through the exploration of taste, it portrays the following key insights:

Celebrating Cultural Diversity Through Culinary Exploration

The story showcases food's power to bridge cultural differences and foster deep understanding and appreciation between individuals from diverse backgrounds. Elena and Marco's journey into each other's culinary heritage demonstrates how taste can serve as a gateway to exploring and celebrating cultural diversity, allowing them to honor their roots while building a life together.

The Intimacy of Shared Experiences

By cooking and enjoying meals together, Elena and Marco cultivate an intimacy that transcends the physical act of eating. This ritual becomes a space for vulnerability, creativity, and mutual support, highlighting how shared experiences, especially those involving the senses, can deepen the emotional bond between partners. The kitchen, as the setting for their culinary adventures, symbolizes the heart of their relationship—a place where love is expressed, nurtured, and sustained.

Fusion as a Metaphor for Relationship Building

Blending Sicilian and Salvadoran cuisines into new fusion dishes represents the dynamic nature of relationships, where differences are acknowledged, celebrated, and woven into a shared identity. This fusion underscores the importance of compromise, creativity, and mutual respect in building a life together, showing that a successful partnership involves creating new traditions and values unique to the couple.

The Role of Traditions in Strengthening Bonds

Establishing their annual "Fusion Feast" shows how creating new traditions can be a cornerstone for relationships, providing a sense of continuity, belonging, and identity. These traditions become markers of their journey together, opportunities to reflect on their growth as a couple and to share their love and heritage with their community, friends, and family.

Culinary Legacy and the Continuity of Love

As Elena and Marco pass their culinary traditions and new creations down to their children, the story touches on legacy and love's enduring nature. This narrative highlights how passions and values can be passed on to future generations, affirming the couple's love and the bridges they've built between their cultures.

A Universal Message of Unity and Love

Elena and Marco beautifully illustrate how love, like cooking, requires patience, experimentation, and willingness to embrace the unknown. It invites readers to consider how their relationships can be enriched by exploring and merging the unique cultural, personal, and emotional flavors each partner brings.

Overall, the narrative conveys a message of unity, love, and the celebration of diversity through the universal language of food. It encourages readers to look beyond surface differences and recognize the profound connections that can be forged when we come together to share the rich flavors of our lives.

Jamie and Alex's Dessert Shop Discovery

In a bustling city where life seldom slows, Jamie and Alex found themselves caught in the whirlwind of their routines. Jamie, a software developer with a penchant for the predictable, and Alex, a budding graphic designer with a taste for adventure, were strangers living parallel lives; their paths had yet to cross. Fate, however, had a different plan that would intertwine their destinies through the unlikely medium of dessert.

A quaint dessert shop tucked away in a quiet corner of the city served as the backdrop for their serendipitous meeting. Jamie, seeking solace in a slice of cheesecake after a long day, and Alex, on a quest to find the perfect raspberry tart, simultaneously reached for the last piece. At that moment, their hands touched, sparking an unexpected connection. Apologies and laughter ensued, leading to a shared table and, eventually, a shared dessert.

As they delved into the cheesecake layers, savoring the creamy texture and the tartness of the raspberry topping, Jamie and Alex began a conversation that meandered through topics as varied as their desserts. Each flavor they tasted became a metaphor for their discoveries about each other—the sweetness of laughter, the zest of new acquaintances, and the richness of forming an unexpected bond.

The dessert shop became their sanctuary, where they could escape the city's hustle and indulge in the simple pleasure of sweet treats and sweeter company. With each visit, they explored new desserts, from the velvety smoothness of chocolate mousse to the spicy warmth of a cinnamon roll. These culinary adventures mirrored the deepening of their relationship as they navigated the complexities of vulnerability, the excitement of new love, and the comfort of found companionship.

Over a piece of cheesecake, what had initially been a chance encounter developed into a love story that drew from the flavors they discovered together. Jamie and Alex learned that love, like dessert, is layered, complex, and capable of evoking a spectrum of emotions. They found that the key to a lasting relationship is the willingness to share, explore, and savor each moment, no matter how fleeting.

Years later, Jamie and Alex returned to the same dessert shop, their hands now entwined, as familiar to each other as the flavors they had once explored with curiosity. They realized that while tastes may evolve and desserts may come and go, the sweetness of their serendipitous meeting and the love that blossomed from it would forever remain a cherished flavor in the journey of their lives.

Poetic Perspective:

In the city's heart, where lights never dim,
Jamie and Alex, on fate's whim.
Found their paths crossed, not by chance,
In a dessert shop's sweet, fragrant expanse.

A cheesecake slice, a tart so fine,
Their hands touched, a sign divine.
From apologies to laughter shared,
A table for two, a moment spared.

Through layers of cheesecake, soft and rich,
An unexpected bond began to stitch.
Flavors mingled, sweet and tart,
Mirroring the budding start.

In this haven of sugar and spice,
They found a sanctuary, a slice of paradise.
With every dessert, a new discovery made,
Of velvety chocolate, of cinnamon's shade.

Their love, like the desserts they savored,
Complex and layered, each moment flavored.
A story of serendipity, of tastes explored,
In the sweetness of connection, love was stored.

The dessert shop, a witness to their tale,
Love that through the simplest pleasures, did sail.
Years later, they returned, hand in hand,
To the place where their love had taken stand.

Jamie and Alex, with flavors so bold,
Understood that love, like desserts, never grows old.
In the sweetness of their serendipitous meet,
Found a love story, oh so sweet.

Through the voyage of life, with its ebb and flow,
They cherished the love that continued to grow.
In the city's heart, under the dimming light,
Their love story remains, forever bright.

Reflection

Through Jamie and Alex's adventures, readers are reminded of the unexpected ways love can enter our lives, often when we least anticipate it. Their narrative celebrates the joy of discovery—of new tastes, new adventures, and new connections—highlighting how, sometimes, it's the simple pleasures that lead to the most profound and lasting bonds. This tale, rich with the flavors of serendipity and sweetness, serves as an ode to the moments that define us and the love that sustains us, calling us to remain open to the possibilities that life and love have to offer.

Jamie and Alex's story, set against the backdrop of a dessert shop encounter, is a multifaceted allegory for love, connection, and the serendipity of life's sweetest moments. This narrative delves into several compelling themes, each interwoven with the sensory experience of taste, to enrich the portrayal of their burgeoning relationship. Here's what it conveys:

Serendipity and the Spontaneity of Life

At its core, the narrative celebrates life's unpredictability. The chance encounter over a piece of cheesecake symbolizes how life's most meaningful connections can arise from the most unexpected circumstances. This theme invites readers to embrace life's spontaneous moments, suggesting that openness to the unexpected can lead to rich, fulfilling experiences and relationships.

The Sensory Experience of Connection

The story explores how shared experiences can deepen emotional connections through the lens of taste and dessert enjoyment. Each dessert Jamie and Alex share catalyzes conversation, discovery, and intimacy, illustrating how shared experiences—be they taste, smell, or sight—can become a medium through which individuals connect and communicate on a deeper level.

The Development of Relationships

Jamie and Alex's journey from strangers to partners highlights the development of relationships, from the initial spark of interest to deeper emotional bonds. Their story suggests that the foundation of a lasting relationship is openness, mutual discovery, and the willingness to explore life together. It portrays love as a layered experience, akin to the desserts they share, filled with complexity, variety, and the potential for endless discovery.

Emotional Resonance of Shared Pleasures

The narrative emphasizes the emotional resonance of shared pleasures and how simple joys, such as enjoying a dessert together, can foster a sense of companionship and happiness. This aspect of the story reflects the importance of finding common ground and delighting in the little things, showcasing how these moments can serve as building blocks for a strong and meaningful relationship.

The Enduring Sweetness of Love

Ultimately, Jamie and Alex's return to the dessert shop years later signifies love's enduring nature and the lasting impact of memories. This concluding scene powerfully recalls that while life may change, the sweetness of moments shared and love discovered remains a constant source of joy and fulfillment.

Through the metaphor of taste and the intimate setting of a dessert shop, Jamie and Alex's story portrays the beauty of serendipitous connections, the depth of relationships formed through shared experiences, and love's enduring sweetness. It encourages readers to savor life's moments, remain open to the unexpected, and cherish the connections that bring flavor and richness to their lives.

Sarah and Lily's Culinary Bridge

In the quiet aftermath of turmoil that had shaken the very foundations of their world, Sarah and her young daughter, Lily, found themselves adrift in a sea of unspoken words and widening distances. The upheaval of a painful divorce had left them both grappling with feelings of loss and disconnection, each retreating into their own shells of hurt and confusion. Amidst this landscape of emotional disarray, they stumbled upon an unexpected bridge back to each other—a bridge built of flour, sugar, and the act of cooking.

The turning point came on a gray, listless afternoon when Sarah, in an attempt to lift the spirits of the house, decided to bake bread. The comforting aroma of yeast and flour drew Lily, who was typically reclusive in her own world of books and drawings, to approach. Hesitantly, she asked if she could help. As their hands met in the dough bowl, kneading and shaping it together, Sarah felt the barriers between them soften. The simple act of making bread—tactile and grounding—became their first shared language in months.

Taking this first step, Sarah made it a point to involve Lily in the kitchen more frequently. Cooking dinners became their daily ritual, a time set apart from the rest of the world's noise. Each recipe they tried, from the simplest of pasta dishes to the more complex ventures into foreign cuisines, served as a lesson in collaboration, patience, and understanding. The emotional chasm that had separated them began to narrow with each meal they prepared, giving way to laughter, stories, and a fresh appreciation for one another's company.

As their culinary adventures grew more ambitious, so did their conversations. Over the delicate process of decorating cupcakes or the triumph of a perfectly roasted chicken, Lily opened up about her feelings—her fears, losses, and hopes. Sarah listened, truly listened, offering her own vulnerabilities in return. Food had become their conduit for healing, a way to express love, apologize, and reassure without the weight of confrontation.

Recognizing the remarkable impact of their kitchen collaborations on their relationship, Sarah and Lily started a new tradition: their weekly "experiment" night. Each Thursday, they would choose a recipe from a different part of the world and explore its history and culture as they cooked. These nights were about more than just food; they were about learning, growing, and celebrating the diversity of human experience together. It was their way of acknowledging that, despite their hardships, the world was still a place of beauty and wonder.

Years later, as Lily grew into a young woman with dreams and passions of her own, the kitchen remained their sacred meeting ground. It was a testament to their journey of reconnecting through the universal language of food. They had learned that it's not just the act of eating that nourishes us but the act of creating and sharing meals that feeds the soul and binds hearts together.

Poetic Perspective:

In the wake of stormy seas, a world apart,
Sarah and Lily sought a fresh start.
Divorce had left its cold, harsh trace,
Yet they found a bridge in the baking space.

A gray afternoon, spirits low,
Sarah decided bread's warmth to bestow.
The aroma of yeast, a call to mend,
Drew Lily close, a hand to lend.

In the bowl, their hands did meet,
Kneading dough, a moment sweet.
A language of flour, sugar, and care,
Softening barriers, layer by layer.

Cooking dinners, a ritual born,
In the kitchen's warmth, their bond reborn.
Pasta dishes, cuisines afar,
A journey of flavors, raising the bar.

Through cupcakes and chickens perfectly roasted,
Lily's fears and dreams were hosted.
Sarah listened, a bond to seal,
In every meal, their healing real.

A tradition emerged, "experiment" nights,
Exploring worlds through culinary flights.
Acknowledging beauty, despite past pain,
In every dish, their love's refrain.

As years unfolded, Lily grew,
In the kitchen, their connection anew.
A sacred space, of memories made,
Proof of the love that stayed.

This culinary bridge, a path to heal,
Revealing love's most authentic feel.
Sarah and Lily, through food's embrace,
Found a recipe for grace.

A narrative of resilience, love's power so bold,
In meals shared, a story told.
A reminder to all, in times of disconnect,
The language of food, hearts to reconnect.

Reflection

Sarah and Lily's story inspires us with the resilience of the human spirit and the power of love to heal and reconnect us, even in the aftermath of life's storms. It underscores the role of culinary adventures in bridging gaps, mending wounds, and forging unbreakable bonds. Through their journey, readers are invited to reflect on the simple yet profound ways food can bring us together, serving as a recipe for reconnection and celebrating the enduring strength of familial love. Sarah and Lily's narrative vividly showcases the healing and transformative power of culinary adventures, especially within family relationships strained by life's adversities. This story dives into several key themes, each contributing to a rich portrayal of how food can become a vital instrument of emotional connection, communication, and healing.

The Healing Power of Shared Activities

At its core, the story highlights the therapeutic potential of engaging in collaborative activities—cooking, in this case—to overcome emotional distances and rebuild relationships. Making bread, which brings Sarah and Lily together for the first time since their familial upheaval, symbolizes the beginning of their emotional healing and reconnection. This theme suggests that everyday activities, especially those involving creativity and sensory engagement, like cooking, can serve as non-verbal platforms for expressing care, fostering understanding, and facilitating meaningful interactions.

Food as a Medium for Communication

The narrative explores how culinary activities transcend mere meal preparation, becoming a language of love and a means of expressing emotions that might be difficult to articulate. Through cooking and sharing meals, Sarah and Lily navigate their feelings of loss, fear, and hope, engaging in conversations that might not have been possible in other contexts. This aspect demonstrates food's unique role in human connection, acting as a catalyst for opening hearts and enabling vulnerable, healing dialogues.

The Creation of New Traditions and Identities

Sarah and Lily's weekly "experiment" night signifies the importance of establishing new traditions in the aftermath of change or turmoil. These traditions provide a sense of continuity and stability, reinforcing the bonds between individuals while also allowing for the creation of a new identity. They portray these culinary traditions as rituals and adventures that celebrate learning, curiosity, and the joy of discovery, reflecting the dynamic nature of relationships and the potential for growth and renewal.

Cultural Exploration and Shared Learning

By exploring recipes from around the world, Sarah and Lily underscore the enriching power of cultural exploration through cuisine. This theme highlights how food can serve as an entry point into different cultures and histories, encouraging mutual learning and appreciation. Such explorations can broaden perspectives, deepen relationships, and foster a sense of curiosity and openness.

The Enduring Bond of Familial Love

Finally, the narrative culminates in a reflection on the enduring strength of the mother-daughter bond, forged and solidified through their culinary journey. Their continuing to cook together even as Lily grows older is a testament to their unwavering love and the ability of relationships to develop and thrive in the face of adversity.

Through Sarah and Lily's journey, readers are invited to consider the profound impact of culinary experiences on emotional healing and relationship building. They portray cooking and sharing meals as acts of love that nourish both the body and the soul, emphasizing the importance of creating spaces for connection, communication, and healing within the framework of family life. This narrative resonates with the universal search for connection and the timeless quest to find and sustain love through the simple yet profound acts of daily living.

Sound: The Echoes of the Heart

The Symphony of Sam and Olivia

In the vibrant weave of their shared life, Sam and Olivia discovered that the most profound connections were often not seen but heard. Amidst the din of their daily existence, the subtle symphony of sound drew them closer, a harmonious blend of laughter, whispered dreams, and the soothing cadence of heartbeats in the quiet of the night.

Their journey began with laughter—a spontaneous, joyous eruption that filled the air around them during their first encounters. Sam's deep, resonant laugh mingled with Olivia's lighter, melodic chuckles, creating a melody of delight that became their unique signature. In those early days, whispers of affection and late-night confessions uttered in hushed tones under the stars formed the foundation of their burgeoning relationship. Each utterance and giggle added layers to their growing collage of moments.

Music soon became the cornerstone of their connection. With his eclectic taste, Sam introduced Olivia to the complex layers of jazz, each note a discovery, a new topic for discussion and mutual appreciation. Olivia, in turn, shared her love for classical music, guiding Sam through the emotional landscapes painted by violins and pianos. Together, they attended concerts, losing themselves in the live renditions of their favorite tracks, the vibrations and rhythms drawing them into a deeper union.

As their relationship deepened, Sam and Olivia learned the value of the quiet moment—the comfortable, companionable silence that enveloped them in moments of contentment or reflection. This shared silence, devoid of awkwardness, spoke volumes of their mutual understanding and acceptance. In these quiet interludes, they found peace, a serene backdrop to the lively soundtrack of their life together.

Years into their journey through life's melodies, the symphony of their home became a testament to their love. The patter of rain on the window, the whistle of a kettle, the soft purring of their cat—all these sounds wove into a comforting melody that signified safety, belonging, and togetherness. The most cherished sound, however, remained the steady rhythm of their heartbeats, a reminder of the life they had built together, a life rich in love, understanding, and shared experiences.

Sam and Olivia remind us that love's essence often lies in the symphony of sounds that accompany our most cherished moments. From laughter and music to the profound silence of companionship, these sounds create a mosaic of memories that define our relationships. Their story underscores the idea that the harmony of shared existence isn't just about the notes played but the spaces between them, the stillness that allows love's melody to resonate more deeply.

Poetic Perspective:

In the realm where whispers dance and heartbeats sing,
Sam and Olivia found love's true offering.
A symphony of moments, soft and clear,
In every laugh, every note, love drew near.

Their laughter mingled in the air, a joyous sound,
A melody of mirth where true love was found.
Whispers under stars, in the night so deep,
Laid the foundation for the love they'd keep.

Jazz and classics, notes floating high and low,
In music's embrace, their affections did grow.
Concerts became their sacred space,
Where in each rhythm, love found its place.

Silent moments, too, held their weight in gold,
In the quiet, their deepest feelings told.
A shared glance, a touch, in the stillness of night,
In these silent songs, their hearts took flight.

Home sounds became their love's refrain,
The rain, the kettle's whistle, a soothing strain.
But above all, their heartbeats' steady hum
Spoke of the life together they'd begun.

Through sounds loud and soft, their love was spun,
In laughter, music, silence, two hearts became one.
Sam and Olivia's story, in harmonies sweet,
A reminder that in love, sound and silence meet.

Reflection

Through the auditory landscape of Sam and Olivia's relationship, readers are encouraged to tune into the sounds that frame their lives, recognizing the music in everyday moments and the stillness in between. This narrative celebrates sound's capacity to evoke emotion, build connections, and enrich the tapestry of human experience with the harmony of love. Sam and Olivia's story offers a rich exploration of how sound—encompassing laughter, music, whispers, and even silence—plays an integral role in developing and deepening romantic relationships. This narrative weaves various auditory experiences to illustrate how sound contributes to emotional intimacy and shared life. Here's a detailed breakdown of the themes and insights portrayed:

The Multifaceted Language of Sound in Love

The narrative highlights sound as a multifaceted language that conveys a broad spectrum of emotions and messages between partners. Laughter represents joy and humor; whispered dreams and confessions symbolize trust and vulnerability; music serves as a medium of mutual discovery and connection; and silence embodies comfort, understanding, and peace. Each sound adds a unique layer to the relationship, enriching the bond between Sam and Olivia.

Sound as a Catalyst for Shared Experiences and Memories

Sam and Olivia's story emphasizes how shared auditory experiences, primarily through music, are powerful catalysts for creating lasting memories and fostering a sense of unity. Their joint exploration of jazz and classical music and their concert attendance illustrates how music can serve as a bridge between individuals, allowing them to experience and appreciate the world from each other's perspectives.

The Significance of Silence in Emotional Intimacy

One of the more profound aspects is the portrayal of silence as an integral component of emotional intimacy. The narrative suggests that the genuine connection between partners can be measured not only by their conversations and laughter but also by their comfort in silence. This silence is depicted as a space for reflection, understanding, and deep emotional connection, highlighting that words are not always necessary to communicate love and support.

The Concept of Home as an Auditory Experience

The story also explores home as not just a physical space but an auditory experience defined by familiar and comforting sounds. Rain, a whistling kettle, and a purring cat are the backdrop to Sam and Olivia's life together, symbolizing safety, belonging, and togetherness. These everyday sounds become markers of their shared existence, contributing to a deeply personal and emotionally resonant sense of home.

The Enduring Power of Love's Symphony

The narrative portrays the enduring power of the symphony of sounds that accompany a relationship over time. Love, in its essence, is a composition of sounds and silences that together create a unique and evolving melody. This melody, with its highs and lows, rhythms and pauses, encapsulates the journey of love in all its complexity and beauty.

Through Sam and Olivia's auditory journey, readers are invited to reflect on the sounds that define their own relationships and appreciate how they contribute to the tapestry of their emotional worlds. The narrative recalls sound's power to evoke emotion, build connections, and enrich our lives with the harmony of love.

Caleb and Ava's Harmonious Discovery

While navigating the early years of their marriage, Caleb and Ava found themselves trapped in the relentless hum of daily responsibilities. The sincere act of listening—to each other and the world around them—had vanished into the background due to the demands of work, family, and the constant buzz of technology.

They stumbled upon the forgotten melody of their love during an autumn retreat to a secluded cabin. Removed from the distractions that cluttered their everyday lives, they began to truly listen again—not just to the words they spoke but to the nuances of tone, the pauses, and the breaths taken in contemplation. Listening opened a new dimension in their relationship, a deeper understanding that words alone could not express.

In the tranquility of the forest, Caleb and Ava rediscovered the calming symphony of the natural world. The rustle of leaves in the gentle breeze, the soft patter of rain on the cabin roof, and the distant call of a lone owl became the backdrop to their renewal. These sounds, once drowned out by the noise of their busy lives, now evoked the inherent beauty of the world and the importance of being present.

In this sanctuary of serenity, they learned to communicate in new ways. A look, a touch, a smile became a wordless conversation, conveying affection, understanding, and support. The background melodies of their surroundings served as a backdrop for this nonverbal communication, which deepened their bond and revealed its unspoken strength.

As days passed, Caleb and Ava found joy in the quiet moments spent together—watching the sunrise in a peaceful embrace, listening to the crackle of the fireplace, and the rhythmic breathing as they lay side by side. These moments, devoid of speech, became the most eloquent expressions of their love, testimonies to the comfort and contentment found in each other's presence.

Returning to the rhythm of their daily lives, Caleb and Ava carried with them the lessons of the cabin—the importance of genuinely listening, finding peace in stillness, and cherishing the natural symphony that life offers. They learned that the world's noise could only overshadow the sound of their love if they allowed it to and that by choosing to listen—to each other and the quiet moments—they could keep the melody of their love vibrant and alive.

Poetic Perspective:

In life's relentless hum and buzz,
Caleb and Ava lost what once was.
A melody of love, soft and clear,
Drowned out by the noise of the everyday sphere.

To a cabin they retreated one autumn day,
Where distractions and clamor faded away.
In the quiet, they began to hear anew,
The subtleties of love that between them grew.

The forest whispered in rustles and sighs,
A symphony of serenity under open skies.
Leaves danced, rain pattered, an owl's call at night,
In nature's embrace, they found renewed light.

A gaze, a touch, a smile without a word,
Spoke volumes of love that their hearts had stirred.
Nonverbal whispers, in the backdrop of peace,
Revealed love's language, and its silent release.

Together, they found joy in moments so still,
Sunrise embraces, warmth by the windowsill.
Side by side, in the night's gentle hold,
Their quiet conversations in love's mold.

Back to the world, with its relentless pace,
They carried the lessons of their tranquil space.
The importance of listening, of being truly present,
In the symphony of life, love's essence is incessant.

The melody of their love, once lost, now reclaimed,
In the harmony of listening, their connection was named.
Caleb and Ava, with love's tune revived,
In the quiet of listening, their love thrived.

Reflection

Caleb and Ava's journey is a poignant reminder that listening is an act of love in a distracted world. It challenges readers to turn down the volume of their lives and tune into the quieter frequencies of connection and understanding, discovering anew the unique sound of love that resonates within each relationship. Caleb and Ava's narrative, set against a tranquil retreat from everyday life, serves as a rich allegory for the complexities of communication and connection within intimate relationships. Through their journey, they illustrate several significant themes and lessons that resonate deeply with the experience of modern love.

The Importance of Active Listening

At its core, the narrative underscores the crucial role of active listening in nurturing and sustaining relationships. Caleb and Ava's initial inability to listen to each other, lost amidst the din of daily obligations and digital distractions, symbolizes a common predicament in contemporary relationships. The story advocates for the intentional practice of active listening, not just to the words spoken but to the feelings, needs, and desires that those words attempt to convey.

Rediscovery Through Silence and Nature

The retreat to a secluded cabin becomes a metaphor for stripping away life's superficial layers to reconnect with the essence of one's partner and the relationship itself. The natural setting emphasizes the restorative power of silence and the symphony of nature, inviting Caleb and Ava—and, by extension, the reader—to rediscover the beauty of the world and each other without the interference of external noise. This theme celebrates the idea that genuine connection often lies beyond verbal communication in the shared appreciation of simple, quiet moments.

Non-verbal communication as a Bonding Force

The story highlights the significance of nonverbal communication in expressing love and affection. Caleb and Ava's renewed relationship, enriched by wordless exchanges such as smiles, touches, and shared glances, illustrates how nonverbal cues can articulate emotions more profoundly than words. The narrative reveals that love is communicated not only through dialogue but also through the silent language of gestures and presence.

The Healing Power of Quietude and Presence

The narrative posits stillness and presence as healing forces that can rejuvenate and deepen relationships. By actively choosing to be present with each other, free from distractions, Caleb and Ava experience a reawakening of their emotional connection. The story suggests that in silence, couples can find a space for introspection, mutual understanding, and emotional intimacy that loud, busy environments often suppress.

Carrying Lessons Back Into the World

Finally, the story offers optimism for integrating the lessons learned during moments of retreat back into the complexities of everyday life. Caleb and Ava's commitment to maintaining the harmony of listening, even in the face of returning to their routines, embodies the hopeful message that the practices of active listening, appreciating nature's quiet beauty, and valuing non-verbal communication can be sustained beyond moments of escape.

Through the lens of Caleb and Ava's experience, the narrative invites readers to reflect on their own relationships, encouraging them to cultivate a deeper level of listening, embrace the quiet moments that foster connection, and remember that the most profound expressions of love often transcend words. It portrays the challenges of modern love and offers a pathway to rediscovering the sounds—and silences—that bind hearts together.

Mia and Harper's Path Through Sound

Mia and Harper, friends since childhood now navigating the complexities of university life together, found the strands of their deep bond beginning to unravel under the weight of unshared thoughts and evolving personal journeys. Conversations that once flowed freely had diminished to surface-level exchanges, leaving a void filled with unspoken anxieties and untold stories. After a particularly sharp disagreement over something as mundane as a forgotten chore, they rediscovered an old vinyl player, a cherished artifact from their youth, offering a path back to understanding and connection.

The heavy silence after their dispute was unexpectedly broken not by words of reconciliation but by an act of reminiscence. In a gesture of peace, Mia carefully set up the vinyl player, an echo from their adolescence, and selected a record they both adored. The initial crackle of the needle touching down was like a collective inhale, a momentary suspension of the tension that had built between them.

As the room began to fill with the rich, warm sounds of classic soul music—a genre that had underscored many of their childhood adventures—something between them began to soften. Side by side, letting the familiar rhythms and lyrics wash over them, Mia and Harper were transported to a simpler time. It was a time when their friendship was defined by endless afternoons of music and comfort, not the misunderstandings and silences that had crept in with adulthood.

This impromptu listening session, sparked by nostalgia, catalyzed deeper communication. As the record spun, the layers of each song encouraged them to peel back their own layers. Harper tentatively shared her fears about the future, her voice barely above the music, and Mia responded with her own insecurities. The act of truly listening to each other, with the music softening the edges of their vulnerabilities, rekindled a sense of mutual understanding and empathy that had been missing.

What began as a nostalgic escape evolved into a ritual. Mia and Harper dedicated time to sitting together, listening to records, and sharing their thoughts and feelings, enveloped in the safety of their shared musical interests. This ritual became their haven, where they could express their deepest worries, celebrate small victories, and offer support without judgment. Through listening—both to the music and each other—they rediscovered the harmony of their friendship.

As they navigated the challenges of university and personal growth, the vinyl player continued to symbolize their enduring bond. Mia and Harper learned that the essence of friendship lies not just in the joyous moments but in the willingness to listen and be present through the discordant ones. Their tale, a reminder of the healing power of music and the importance of listening, is a gentle reminder that genuine connection often requires tuning in to the unspoken melodies of each other's hearts.

Poetic Perspective:

In university's labyrinth, where paths diverge and twist,
Mia and Harper's bond faced trials, amidst
The clutter of evolving lives, a friendship strained,
Until an old vinyl player, a memory retained,
Became the unexpected bridge back to their shared domain.

A dispute left silence heavy, a chasm wide,
Yet Mia chose music over pride.
With a record's crackle, tension paused,
In classic soul's embrace, their discord defrosted.

Side by side, as melodies flowed,
A journey back in time, to when their friendship glowed.
Music, the backdrop of their youth, now the key,
Unlocking doors to memories, setting their spirits free.

Nostalgia's wave led to deeper shores,
Where fears and dreams could voice, doors open to explore.
In vulnerability shared, a new understanding born,
The music softening shadows, their friendship reborn.

This ritual of records, of listening, became their rite,
A sanctuary for their bond, through day and night.
In each lyric and pause, a language found,
Where support and love could unbound.

Through the vinyl's spin, their friendship's melody played,
Testimony of the power of listening, a foundation relayed.
Mia and Harper, in harmony once more,
Discovered that true connection requires the courage to explore.

Their story, a melody of resilience and care,
Reminds us that friendship's essence is always there.
In the act of listening, a sacred space,
Where understanding and empathy interlace.

Through sound, through silence, their bond did mend,
Proving that friendship, like music, finds its rhythm in the end.

Reflection

Through Mia and Harper, readers are encouraged to consider the transformative power of listening in all relationships. Their story illustrates that amidst life's distractions, finding a common frequency to connect can turn dissonance into harmony, reinforcing the timeless truth that listening—to music, to each other—is where understanding and deep connection truly begin. Mia and Harper's story explores the complexities of maintaining a deep, long-standing friendship amidst the inevitable changes and challenges of growing up. Several key themes emerge through their journey of sound's profound impact, each offering insights into friendship dynamics, communication, and mutual understanding.

The Impact of Unspoken Struggles on Relationships

The narrative begins by portraying how unvoiced anxieties, pressures, and personal growth can create distance in a close relationship. Mia and Harper's transition from effortless communication to surface-level exchanges underscores a common phenomenon in friendships: the failure to share deeper feelings leads to disconnection. This aspect of the story reflects the challenges of keeping the essence of a relationship intact as individuals evolve.

The Power of History and Nostalgia

Rediscovering the old vinyl player is pivotal in the narrative, symbolizing the power of shared history and nostalgia in rekindling connections. This element highlights how revisiting common memories and experiences can bridge gaps in understanding and closeness, reminding both characters—and the reader—of the foundational experiences that forged their bond.

Listening as a Form of Emotional Support

Central to Mia and Harper's reconciliation is the theme of listening, not just in the literal sense of enjoying music together but in the figurative sense of truly hearing and understanding each other's fears and hopes. The narration emphasizes that genuine listening involves more than just hearing words; it requires empathy, openness, and a willingness to engage with another's emotional world. This act of listening becomes a medium through which Mia and Harper navigate their misunderstandings and rediscover their connection.

The Role of Rituals in Sustaining Relationships

Establishing a new ritual—dedicating time to listen to records and share personal thoughts—illustrates the importance of intentional practices in maintaining and deepening relationships. This recurring act of coming together in a space of mutual comfort and safety allows Mia and Harper to rebuild their communication and support for one another, showing how rituals can serve as anchors in a friendship, providing continuity and a sense of shared identity.

The Importance of Presence and Mutual Understanding

Ultimately, the story portrays the significance of being present with and for each other, even (or especially) when life's noise threatens to drown out the essence of the relationship. Mia and Harper's journey back to a harmonious friendship through music and listening serves as a metaphor for reconnecting with those we value. It underscores the idea that true friendship requires effort, understanding, and, most importantly, the willingness to be truly present in each other's lives.

The narrative conveys to readers that the essence of enduring friendships lies in the ability to listen—to the said and unsaid—and to remain attuned to each other's emotional frequencies, regardless of life's discordances. Through Mia and Harper's story, we are reminded of the transformative power of listening and the enduring strength of connections forged in understanding and shared experiences.

Vision Beyond Sight
Theo and Riley's Voyage for Sight

Theo and Riley's story unfolds in the vibrant hues of mutual discovery and the profound, intimate process of truly "seeing" one another beyond the surface. Their connection begins not with a spark of physical attraction but with the exciting realization that each harbors a world within them waiting to be understood and appreciated.

Their meeting was unmarked by an exchange of glances across a crowded room but by the discovery of a shared volunteer project, where their task was to create a garden for the visually impaired. Working side by side, they communicated through the language of texture, scent, and sound, guiding each other's hands to plant, feel, and appreciate the beauty beyond the visual.

As Theo and Riley's friendship deepened, so did their appreciation for the nuances of the world around them. An avid photographer, Riley began sharing her worldview through her lens, capturing moments for their aesthetic appeal, the stories they told, and the emotions they evoked. With a keen interest in literature, Theo introduced Riley to the vivid landscapes of poetry and prose, where words painted pictures that transcended sight.

Through their shared experiences, Theo and Riley learned the art of seeing—beyond mere observation to a deep engagement with the essence of things. They discovered that truly seeing someone is understanding the myriad colors that paint their thoughts, the shadows that flicker in their fears, and the light that shines in their dreams. It was a process of unveiling, peeling back layers to reveal the raw and beautiful truth of one another's being.

This path taught them that vision is not solely the domain of the eyes but a multilayered perception that engages all senses and the heart. They learned to see each other in moments of joy and brightness and in the depths of shadows and silence, recognizing the strength and vulnerability that lie within. This deeper vision forged a profound and unshakeable bond rooted in mutual respect and understanding.

As their relationship evolved, Theo and Riley continued to explore the world through each other's perspectives, each moment of seeing and being seen deepening their connection. They created a shared mosaic of expressions that celebrated the richness of life beyond the visual, reinforcing the idea that the most meaningful connections engage the soul as much as the senses.

Poetic Perspective:

In domains where sight does not dictate,
Theo and Riley found a gate.
To worlds unseen, where hearts perceive
The depths of souls, in webs they weave.

Not in the glance of fleeting eyes,
But in a project 'neath open skies,
A garden for those whose sight had fled,
Together, their hands and spirits led.

With texture, scent, and whispers low,
They touched the world's soft, secret glow.
Riley, through lenses, caught life's dance,
Theo, with words, gave thought a glance.

Beyond mere sight, their vision grew,
To see the heart, the soul, the true.
In each other's dreams and fears, they delved,
A bond in shared sight, marvelously helved.

Not just with eyes, but with the heart,
They learned to see, to set apart.
The light and dark within each soul,
To understand, to see the whole.

Their love, a world interlaced
With colors, shadows, and light embraced.
Through shared views, a deeper connection found,
In sight beyond sight, their hearts were bound.

As their world expanded, so did their creed,
In a mosaic of moments, love's seed.
Celebrating life's unseen grace,
In the art of seeing, their souls embrace.

Thus, Theo and Riley, in silent accord,
Discovered love's true, unseen chord.
In the voyage for sight, beyond the visual plane,
Their hearts' eyes opened, forever to remain.

Reflection

Theo and Riley's story reminds readers that the essence of connection lies in the ability to truly see one another—to look beyond the exterior and connect with the inner landscapes of thoughts, emotions, and dreams. The narrative invites readers to reconsider their perceptions of seeing and being seen, encouraging a deeper, more holistic approach to understanding and valuing the people in their lives. Through their journey, we are reminded that the most profound form of vision perceives the beauty of the soul, the complexities of the mind, and the myriad emotions that define our shared humanity. Theo and Riley's story illuminates the path to a deeper connection that transcends the physical to touch the essence of being.

Theo and Riley's narrative, "Vision Beyond Sight," delves into the profound concept of seeing in all its depth and complexity, particularly within the context of human connections. This story elegantly unfolds the journey of two individuals who learn to perceive each other and the world around them in ways beyond mere physical sight, emphasizing emotional, intellectual, and spiritual dimensions of vision. Here's a comprehensive analysis of the key themes and messages expressed:

The Multidimensional Nature of Seeing

At the story's heart is the exploration of seeing as a multidimensional experience that involves more than just the physical act of looking. It highlights how true vision encompasses understanding, empathy, and a deep appreciation for another's inner world. By engaging in activities that require non-visual senses, Theo and Riley learn to appreciate the beauty that isn't immediately visible, suggesting that profound connections are formed when we perceive with our hearts and minds as well as our eyes.

Connection Through Shared Experiences and Interests

The narrative emphasizes the importance of shared experiences—such as creating a sensory garden and exploring art and literature—in building rich and meaningful connections. These shared endeavors allow Theo and Riley to communicate and understand each other in ways that words alone cannot achieve. This theme underscores the idea that relationships deepen through mutual exploration and the exchange of perspectives, leading to a more nuanced understanding of each other.

Emotional Intimacy and Vulnerability

As Theo and Riley's relationship deepens, so does their emotional intimacy, characterized by their willingness to be vulnerable and see each other in moments of strength and weakness. This aspect of the story illustrates how true vision involves recognizing and embracing the full spectrum of another's humanity—their hopes, fears, joys, and sorrows. It suggests that deep connections are nurtured by seeing the best in each other and understanding and accepting the complexities and imperfections.

The Role of Art and Creativity in Perception

Art and creativity serve as vital conduits for seeing beyond the surface. Riley's photography and Theo's passion for literature are depicted not just as hobbies but as means of expressing and sharing their unique visions of the world. This theme reflects how art and creativity can open our eyes to new ways of seeing, encouraging us to appreciate the beauty and depth in the world and each other.

The Transformative Power of True Vision

Ultimately, the story conveys the transformative power of developing a genuine vision that appreciates the unseen qualities that define us as individuals. Theo and Riley's journey from mere acquaintances to deeply connected partners showcases the potential for transformation when individuals genuinely open themselves to see and understand each other on a profound level.

"Theo and Riley's Journey of Seeing" invites readers to reconsider their approach to seeing the people in their lives. It encourages an exploration of the deeper aspects of vision, suggesting that the most meaningful connections stem from our ability to perceive and appreciate the invisible qualities that make each person unique. This narrative reminds us of the beauty and complexity of human connection, achieved through the holistic act of truly seeing one another.

Eliza and Jordan's Path to Clarity

In the serene embrace of a dense forest, where light filters through the canopy in dappled patterns, Eliza and Jordan found themselves participants in a wilderness retreat designed to strip away the distractions of the modern world and foster a deeper connection with nature—and inadvertently, with each other.

Eliza, an urbanite graphic designer, and Jordan, a conservationist, initially saw the world through vastly different lenses. Eliza's vision was shaped by the vibrant chaos of city life and digital landscapes, while Jordan found clarity in the natural patterns and tranquility of the wild. Their differing perspectives on vision—what it means to see and what is worthy of our gaze—became the first point of contention and the seed for something more profound.

Part of the retreat involved a workshop titled "The Art of Seeing," where participants were encouraged to explore the forest without the goal-oriented mindset that typically guides their perception. Guided by the soft-spoken facilitator, they were taught to observe the minutiae of their surroundings—the way light plays on leaves, the intricate designs of bark, and the dance of shadows and light. For Eliza, this exercise transformed her understanding of vision; it was no longer about seeking out the grandiose but appreciating the beauty in subtlety.

As the retreat progressed, Eliza and Jordan were drawn together by their shared discoveries. A quiet acknowledgment of a bird's song or mutual admiration for how the sunlight fractured through the canopy became moments of connection. They learned to communicate through these profound visions, each moment of mutual recognition building a bridge between their worlds.

Through their shared experiences in the forest, Eliza and Jordan began to see each other in a new light. Eliza saw beyond Jordan's initial reluctance to his deep reverence for nature and knowledge of the forest's rhythms. Jordan, in turn, recognized Eliza's keen eye for design not as a purely urban skill but as a form of vision that could capture and celebrate the beauty of the natural world in ways he had never considered.

By the retreat's end, Eliza and Jordan had forged an unexpected and profound connection. They had journeyed from contention to understanding, learning to appreciate the world around them and each other through a new lens of vision. Their final evening was spent watching the stars emerge through the gaps in the canopy, a moment of silent clarity and depth they had taken in together.

Poetic Perspective:

In the forest's heart, where light and shadow play,
Eliza and Jordan found a different way.
A retreat from chaos, from urban sprawl,
To learn in nature's embrace, to hear its silent call.

From city's rush to the wild's serene grace,
Their visions clashed in this new space.
But as leaves whispered and bark told tales,
Their eyes opened to what true sight entails.

"The Art of Seeing," a path to explore,
Beyond the obvious, to something more.
Eliza learned to see the world anew,
In the dance of light, in the morning dew.

Together they wandered, in silence and talk,
Learning each other's ways, in the forest's gentle walk.
A song of a bird, sunlight through trees,
In shared wonder, they found ease.

Eliza, with her designer's eye,
Saw nature's palette, vast and high.
Jordan, with his conservationist's heart,
Showed her the wild, art's counterpart.

In the retreat's cocoon, their contention eased,
In nature's classroom, their spirits were pleased.
Under the stars' watchful eyes,
They found a clarity, a prize.

No longer divided by city and leaf,
Their connection grew, firm in belief.
That in the art of truly seeing,
Lies the path to being, to freeing.

Eliza and Jordan, in nature's hold,
Discovered a vision, bold and untold.
In the serenity of the forest's embrace,
They found clarity, a shared space.

Reflection

Returning to their respective lives, Eliza and Jordan carried with them the lessons of the forest—the understanding that vision has multiple layers and is deeply personal. Truly seeing requires patience, openness, and the willingness to perceive the world and its people with curiosity and empathy. Their story is a testament to the transformative power of vision, inviting readers to look beyond the surface, find connection in moments of discovery, and appreciate how we see and understand the world and each other. This tale explores the compelling themes of perception, connection, and the transformative power of nature. Through Eliza and Jordan's experiences, the story delves into several vital insights about literal and metaphorical vision and how these insights facilitate a deeper understanding and bond between individuals.

Perception Shaped by Environment

The story introduces two characters, Eliza and Jordan, whose perceptions of the world are shaped by their environments—urban and natural, respectively. This contrast sets the stage for exploring how our surroundings influence our way of seeing the world and, by extension, our relationships with others. It suggests that our vision is not just a sensory experience but is also colored by our interactions, experiences, and the contexts in which we find ourselves.

The Art of Seeing

The workshop within the story is a pivotal moment for both characters, emphasizing that vision extends beyond mere observation to include appreciation, understanding, and emotional engagement. This narrative element highlights that true sight involves seeing beyond the surface to appreciate the intricacies and beauty of the world around us, encouraging a shift from a goal-oriented perception to one that values the journey and the details along the way.

Experience as a Medium for Connection

Eliza and Jordan's evolving relationship illustrates how shared experiences, particularly those engaging with the natural world, can be a powerful medium for forging connections. Their moments of mutual recognition and appreciation—whether for a bird's song or the play of light through the trees—demonstrate how everyday experiences can bridge individual differences and foster a sense of unity and understanding.

The Transformation of Vision

Throughout the retreat, both characters transform their way of perceiving their environment and each other. This change symbolizes the broader potential for individuals to evolve their perceptions through openness to new experiences and the willingness to see from another's perspective. The narrative suggests that such transformations in vision can lead to deeper, more meaningful relationships based on mutual respect and appreciation.

The Lasting Impact of Expanded Perception

Finally, the story reflects on the lasting impact of the characters' shared experiences and expanded perception as they return to their lives with a newfound appreciation for the subtleties of both the natural world and human connection. This outcome underscores the narrative's core message: that by broadening our vision and embracing the full spectrum of our sensory experiences, we can enhance our understanding of the world and enrich our relationships with others.

The narrative invites readers to reconsider their perceptions and engagement with the world and the people around them. It celebrates the power of nature to inspire change, the importance of shared experiences in building connections, and the transformative potential of genuinely seeing and appreciating the world in all its complexity and beauty.

Priya and Max's Palette of Understanding

In the heart of a vibrant art studio filled with the scent of oil paints and turpentine, Priya and Max embarked on a collaborative art project that challenged their perceptions and deepened their connection in ways neither anticipated. Priya, a seasoned painter known for her vibrant landscapes, and Max, a sculptor who worked with reclaimed materials, were paired for an exhibition intended to blur the boundaries between their mediums.

Their collaboration began with skepticism. Priya's world was color and form, where vision played out across canvases in bold strokes and delicate hues. Max's realm was tactile, rooted in the weight, texture, and form of physical materials. Their first attempts to merge these worlds were clumsy, marked by a struggle to find a common language encompassing sight and touch.

As they spent hours in the studio, something shifted. Priya introduced Max to visual texture, showing him how colors and brushstrokes could evoke a sense of touch. Max, in turn, guided Priya's hands over his sculptures, showcasing how form and material could tell stories as vivid as any painting. Through this exchange, they began seeing their mediums through a new lens, discovering the nuances of vision and perception they had previously overlooked.

The breakthrough came when they decided to create a piece that neither could have envisioned alone—a sculpture that seemed to emerge from a canvas, where painted colors gave way to tangible forms. This piece, a remarkable fusion of exploration, symbolized the merging of their perspectives, creating a visual experience that invited viewers to both look and feel.

Through their collaboration, Priya and Max learned that vision is more than what meets the eye; it's an invitation to explore, understand, and connect with the world in different ways. True sight involves a willingness to see beyond one's own perspective, embrace the unknown, and find harmony in diversity.

When the exhibition opened, visitors were drawn to Priya and Max's piece, captivated by its unique fusion of form and color, texture and space. Standing beside their work, Priya and Max realized that their love for art had taught them more than how to blend painting and sculpture; it had opened their eyes to the depth of connection possible when individuals dare to see the world through each other's eyes.

When they returned to their individual practices, Priya and Max carried with them the lessons of their collaboration. They approached their art with renewed curiosity and openness, recognizing that vision is not just a solitary act of perception but a dialogue—a shared exploration of the world's beauty and complexity.

Poetic Perspective:

In the studio's embrace, where colors breathe and sculptures stand,
Priya and Max embarked, side by side, hand in hand.
A painter and sculptor, set in their ways,
Found themselves at the crossroads of art's intricate maze.

Priya's world was a canvas bright,
Max's realm, a tactile night.
Their early attempts, a disjointed song,
Struggled to find the place where they belong.

But as time unfurled its guiding hand,
Together in the studio, they took a stand.
Priya taught Max of visual feel,
Max showed Priya that form could heal.

A sculpture and canvas, together they fused,
A symbol of their barriers, gently bruised.
This piece, evidence of their journey's core,
Invited the world to feel, to explore.

Through paint and texture, form and light,
They learned that vision could take flight.
Beyond the eye, into the realm of soul,
Where understanding and connection toll.

The exhibition opened, their piece took the stage,
A fusion of their work, the turning page.
Beside their creation, they understood,
Their collaboration had unearthed something good.

Back in their corners of art's wide field,
The lessons of their union, a protective shield.
They approached their work with a new-found sight,
For in their journey, they found a new light.

In the melding of their art, a dialogue born,
A shared exploration of the morn.
Priya and Max, through vision's wide door,
Discovered a world worth seeing more.

In this tale of art, of sight, of feel,
We find a truth that is incredibly real.
The beauty of seeing, a shared endeavor,
Brings souls together, forever and ever.

Reflection

Priya and Max's story invites readers to contemplate the expansive nature of vision, encouraging an understanding that extends beyond the visual to include the tactile, the emotional, and the collaborative. It's a narrative that celebrates the transformative power of shared creativity and the endless possibilities that emerge when we allow ourselves to see and be seen by others. Set within the creative confluence of visual and tactile art, the story offers a rich exploration of vision, collaboration, and the expansive potential of artistic expression. Through Priya and Max's journey, the narrative delves into several profound themes:

The Interplay Between Different Modes of Perception

The story spotlights the dynamic interplay between the visual and tactile, challenging the conventional boundaries that define artistic mediums. Priya's immersion in the world of colors and forms contrasts with Max's engagement with the physicality and texture of materials, setting the stage for a broader discussion about how we perceive and interpret the world around us. This theme suggests that vision, while predominantly associated with the eyes, is deeply interconnected with our other senses, enriching our understanding and experience of art and life.

Collaboration as a Catalyst for Growth

Priya and Max's initial skepticism towards their collaborative project evolves into a profound mutual understanding and respect, highlighting the narrative's emphasis on collaboration as a vehicle for personal and artistic growth. Their journey from contention to synergy exemplifies how working closely with others, especially those with differing perspectives can push individuals to explore beyond their comfort zones, leading to groundbreaking and innovative creations.

Vision Beyond Sight

Central to the story is the exploration of vision beyond mere sight—to see is to look, feel, understand, and connect. Through their artistic partnership, Priya and Max learn to appreciate the unseen textures and stories within their works, broadening the scope of what it means to truly "see." This aspect of the narrative invites readers to consider the depth of their perception, encouraging a more holistic approach to observing the world that integrates sight with touch, emotion, and intellectual engagement.

The Power of Shared Vision in Creating New Realities

The creation of their joint art piece—a sculpture emerging from a painted canvas—serves as a metaphor for the transformative power of shared vision. This fusion of their artistic expressions into a singular, cohesive work symbolizes the potential to create new realities when diverse perspectives and talents are harmonized. It's a testament to the idea that unity in diversity can lead to outcomes that are greater than the sum of their parts.

The Enduring Impact of Artistic Exploration

Lastly, the story reflects the enduring impact of Priya and Max's collaboration on their artistic practices. Their experience underscores the lasting value of openness, curiosity, and the willingness to engage with different perspectives. By carrying these lessons beyond the studio, they embody the narrative's broader message about the continuous journey of discovery and understanding that defines art and life.

The narrative celebrates the confluence of visual and tactile art and serves as a broader allegory for the complexities of human perception and connection. Through Priya and Max's story, readers are encouraged to explore the rich tapestry of sensory experiences, embrace collaboration and diversity, and see vision as a broadly creative, interpretive, and connective process.

Smell's Essence of Affinity

Liam and Sofia's Olfactory Odyssey

In a quaint town between rolling hills and verdant fields, Liam and Sofia embarked on a journey of discovery to uncover the profound impact of scent on memory, connection, and love. Liam, a botanist with a passion for the aromatic wonders of the plant world, and Sofia, a perfumer who crafted scents that evoked deep emotions and memories, crossed paths at a local market.

Their first encounter was not visual but olfactory. Amidst the busy market, Sofia's unique blend of lavender and cedarwood, a scent she was testing for her new perfume line, caught Liam's attention. They struck up a conversation about the fragrance and the memories and emotions it evoked. Liam shared stories of lavender fields he'd studied while Sofia spoke of the art of capturing emotions in a bottle.

Inspired by their initial meeting, Liam and Sofia began collaborating, blending their expertise to create a series of scents inspired by nature's aromas. Each scent aimed to evoke not just memories but to forge new ones. Their partnership was a dance of scientific knowledge and artistic creativity, with each fragrance telling a story of the earth, the plants, and the profound depth of smell.

As they delved deeper into their project, Liam and Sofia discovered a new connection through the scents they created. They learned that smell, often overlooked, has the unique power to transport us back in time to moments of joy, sadness, and everything in between. They explored how certain aromas could comfort, invigorate, or soothe, weaving an invisible thread between people and their memories.

Their collaboration culminated in an exhibition not of sights, but of scents. Visitors were invited to journey through a curated landscape of fragrances, each station designed to unearth different memories and emotions. Liam and Sofia watched as people closed their eyes, inhaled, and were momentarily transported elsewhere, their faces reflecting a myriad of emotions. It was a testament to the evocative power of scent and its ability to connect us to our past, our desires, and each other.

The exhibition's success was not only a professional triumph for Liam and Sofia but also a personal journey of discovery. Through their collaboration, they deepened their understanding of the olfactory world and formed a connection that transcended the professional. They realized that their partnership had blossomed into something more, a relationship built on shared passions, discoveries, and the invisible yet palpable language of scent.

Poetic Perspective:

In a quaint town where fields and hills embrace,
Liam and Sofia found a shared space.
Not through sight but scent, their paths entwined,
In the market's hustle, a fragrant find.

Sofia's blend of wood and flower caught the air,
Liam, drawn by scent, found something rare.
Tales of lavender fields and emotions caught,
In perfumes and plants, a shared thought.

Together they embarked on an olfactory quest,
To capture nature's aromas, in their zest.
Each scent a story, a memory to unfold,
A dance of science and art, beautifully bold.

Deeper they delved into the essence of smell,
Finding in each aroma a powerful spell.
To evoke, to comfort, to transport the mind,
In the power of scent, a bond defined.

An exhibition of fragrances, not of sights,
Invited guests to explore olfactory delights.
Each inhale a journey, a moment relived,
In the power of scent, their art thrived.

The success of their venture, both professional and sweet,
Marked a beginning, where heart and passion meet.
In the language of scent, a connection found,
A partnership in aroma, profoundly bound.

Liam and Sofia, through scents explored,
Discovered a union, in essence stored.
In the olfactory odyssey, their love did bloom,
In the world of aromas, their hearts found room.

Reflection

We invite readers to explore the often-underestimated sense of smell and its profound impact on human emotions, memories, and connections. Through Liam and Sofia's journey, the narrative illuminates how scents can serve as powerful conduits for emotional expression, recalling the past and shaping new experiences. It celebrates the idea that amidst our visually dominated world, the olfactory sense offers a unique pathway to deepen our connections with the world and each other, reminding us of the intricate and invisible ways in which we are interlinked.

The narrative delves into the profound and often underappreciated sense of smell, illustrating its capacity to evoke memories, forge emotional connections, and enhance interpersonal relationships. Through Liam and Sofia's creative and scientific collaboration, the story explores several critical themes related to olfaction and its place in human life.

The Evocative Power of Scent

The story's central theme is scent's extraordinary ability to transport individuals across time and space, triggering vivid memories and emotions with just a whiff. Liam and Sofia's journey into creating a series of nature-inspired scents underscores how specific smells can instantly recall past experiences, both personal and universal, highlighting scent's role as a direct line to emotional centers in the brain.

Collaboration Across Disciplines

The narrative highlights the fruitful outcomes that can arise from interdisciplinary collaboration. Liam's botanical expertise and Sofia's perfumery skills combine to create something neither could achieve alone—a collection of fragrances that tell stories and evoke emotions. This theme speaks to the broader idea that bridging different fields of knowledge and practice can lead to innovative and meaningful discoveries.

Scent as a Language

Through their work, Liam and Sofia discover that scent can be a unique language for expressing complex emotions and narratives. The story illustrates how this olfactory language can communicate subtleties and nuances that words might fail to capture, offering a non-verbal mode of expression that is deeply personal and universally understood.

The Role of Scent in Human Connection

A significant message of the story is the role of scent in creating and deepening human connections. The exhibition, where visitors experience a journey through scents, metaphorically demonstrates how shared sensory experiences can unite people, evoke shared humanity, and foster empathy. It's a poignant reminder of how personal and collective memories can be accessed and relived through the sense of smell.

Personal Growth and Discovery

Lastly, the narrative explores the personal growth and discovery experienced by Liam and Sofia through their collaborative project. Beyond professional achievement, their journey leads to mutual understanding and connection, illustrating how working closely with another person can lead to unexpected personal insights and blossoming new relationships.

"Scents of Connection" invites readers to reconsider the importance of the sense of smell in their own lives, encouraging a deeper appreciation for how scents shape our memories, emotions, and connections with others. By weaving together the science of olfaction with the art of perfumery, the story celebrates scent's invisible yet powerful impact on the tapestry of human experience, highlighting its capacity to enrich and deepen our understanding of the world and each other.

Ella and Kai's Natural Connection

Ella and Kai's story unfolds on a university campus, where paths cross and destinies intertwine in natural and unexpected ways. Without perfumes or colognes, their tale is one of raw attraction, guided by the invisible force of pheromones—natural scents that speak to our instincts, drawing us together through an unspoken language of chemistry.

Their initial meeting was understated. During a biology class, they found themselves drawn to work together, a choice that seemed guided by convenience but was influenced by an underlying chemistry they couldn't yet identify. It was an automatic connection, a natural gravitation towards each other that neither could logically explain.

As biology majors interested in human behavior, Ella and Kai explored pheromones in a class project. Their research uncovered the world of natural scents and their role in human attraction. This led to a realization about their connection, suggesting that their initial draw was perhaps less about choice and more about biological signals their bodies were unconsciously sending and receiving.

Curious about pheromones' influence on their attraction, Ella and Kai conducted an experiment. They avoided all scented products, allowing their natural scents to remain unmasked. In the following days, they noticed an intensified closeness, a deeper instinctive pull that transcended their relationship's visual or verbal aspects.

This experimentation brought them closer, not just through the biological affirmation of their attraction but through the conversations and shared vulnerabilities it opened up. They discussed their fears, hopes, and dreams, finding their connection deepened with each layer of understanding. Their attraction, initiated by the subtle language of scent, evolved into an emotional and intellectual bond.

Ella and Kai's relationship of natural connections fortified their understanding of life's invisible forces. They found a partner who complemented and challenged each other, someone who resonated with their essence on every level. Their love story, initiated by the silent signals of pheromones, grew to encompass how humans connect emotionally, intellectually, and spiritually.

Poetic Perspective:

In the calm of a sprawling campus green,
Ella and Kai's tale quietly took scene.
No perfumes worn, no scents applied,
Yet towards each other, they instinctively spied.

In biology's realm, they found their start,
Drawn together by an unseen art.
A natural force, a chemistry pure,
Guiding their paths, subtly sure.

Curiosity piqued, they delved into study,
Uncovering pheromones, their attraction less muddy.
An experiment ensued, all artificial scents ceased,
In their natural essence, their attraction increased.

This journey of discovery, of scent and soul,
Brought them closer, made them whole.
Through shared fears, hopes, and dreams,
Their bond deepened, or so it seems.

Ella and Kai, in their essence entwined,
Found in each other a match aligned.
Their love, beyond the silent chemistry,
Grew in depth, in emotional symmetry.

In the world of scents, unseen but felt,
They found a connection, heartfelt.
Ella and Kai, through nature's cue,
Discovered love, honest and true.

Reflection

This narration highlights natural scents' remarkable and often overlooked role in forming human bonds. Through Ella and Kai's journey, the narrative invites readers to consider the primal aspects of attraction that operate beneath our conscious awareness, shaping our relationships in ways we might not fully understand.

Their story celebrates love's complexity, reminding us that while the initial spark between individuals might be rooted in biology, a relationship's depth and endurance are cultivated through mutual respect, shared experiences, and the continual effort to see and understand each other beyond the surface. It underscores the idea that the most profound connections embrace the entirety of our being—mind, body, and soul.

The narrative delves into the fascinating, often invisible world of human pheromones and their impact on attraction. It uses Ella and Kai's relationship as a lens to explore broader themes of connection, compatibility, and the foundations of love. The story weaves scientific curiosity with the personal journey of two individuals discovering the depth of their bond, offering insights into several key aspects of human relationships.

The Role of Pheromones in Attraction

At its core, the story illuminates the biological underpinnings of attraction, highlighting the role of pheromones—chemical signals emitted by the human body that can influence the behavior and perception of others. By focusing on Ella and Kai's attraction and their experiment with natural scents, the narrative highlights how our biological makeup plays a significant, albeit often subconscious, role in drawing us to potential partners. This theme invites readers to reflect on the initial factors that spark connections between people, suggesting that attraction extends beyond conscious choice or physical appearance.

The Intersection of Science and Personal Experience

Ella and Kai's journey from classmates to partners, catalyzed by their shared interest in the science of pheromones, underscores the enriching potential of intellectual collaboration and curiosity in forming deep connections. Their story bridges the gap between academic inquiry and personal experience, illustrating how exploring scientific phenomena can lead to greater self-awareness and understanding of one's relationships. It emphasizes that love and attraction are not just matters of the heart but are also deeply intertwined with the mysteries of the human body and mind.

Experimentation and Discovery in Relationships

The personal experiment that Ella and Kai undertake—eschewing all artificial scents to explore their natural attraction—metaphorically represents the broader process of discovery and understanding in relationships. This aspect of the story suggests that getting to know another person deeply often involves experimentation, openness, and a willingness to explore uncharted territories together. It highlights the value of curiosity and mutual exploration in building a solid foundation for a relationship.

A Multilayered Natural Connection

While the narrative begins with a focus on the biological basis of attraction, it evolves to explore the emotional, intellectual, and spiritual dimensions of Ella and Kai's connection. This evolution reflects the story's broader message: true compatibility and lasting bonds are built on a complex interplay of factors, including shared values, interests, and a deep understanding of each other's inner worlds. The story illustrates that the most profound relationships engage all aspects of our being, transcending the initial chemistry to embrace a fuller spectrum of connection.

Compatibility Beyond the Physical

Finally, "Essence of Affinity" invites readers to consider the essence of compatibility and the role of innate, perhaps even primal, factors in shaping our closest relationships. By highlighting Ella and Kai's natural connection, underscored by their biological compatibility and deepened through shared experiences and values, the narrative suggests that the strongest bonds are those formed through a combination of natural affinity and conscious commitment to understanding and supporting each other.

Through Ella and Kai's story, readers are encouraged to appreciate the subtle, often overlooked factors that influence relationships and recognize the importance of exploring and nurturing connections on multiple levels. The narrative celebrates the beauty of discovering and embracing the natural affinities that draw us together and proposes that such discoveries can lead to deeper, more meaningful partnerships.

A World Intertwined by Aromas

In the mosaic of a small coastal town, where the sea's rhythm meets the earth's lush embrace, a world of lives converge, each thread colored by its unique scent, weaving a narrative that captures the essence of human connection and the invisible ties that bind us.

Marina, a marine biologist, carries the scent of the ocean in her being—the crisp, salty air mingled with a hint of seaweed and sand. Her life's work, dedicated to conserving marine wonders, has imbued her with an aroma that speaks of vast horizons and deep, mysterious waters. Her scent draws people to her, inspiring a shared reverence for the sea's beauty and crucial role in our collective story.

Luca, a gardener nurturing the earth's richness in the heart of the town, is enveloped by the aroma of soil and green growth. His hands, forever marked by the earth, release a fragrance of freshly turned soil, wildflowers, and the first rain, telling tales of rebirth and connection to the land. His essence reminds others of nature's cycles—growth, bloom, and renewal—inviting them into a deeper relationship with the earth that sustains us all.

Amira, a perfumer whose ancestry is steeped in the art of fragrance, blends scents that capture the town's spirit. Her creations are not merely perfumes but stories bottled up, each scent a chapter that evokes memories, dreams, and the subtle emotions that color our days. With every fragrance she crafts, Amira weaves together the individual essences of the town's inhabitants, creating a collective aroma of unity, diversity, and the invisible bonds of community.

Once a year, the town hosts a festival celebrating its cultural heritage and the natural world surrounding it. In this carnival of scents, Marina, Luca, Amira, and others come together, their aromas blending into a symphony of scents that tells the story of their interwoven lives. The festival becomes a sensory journey through the landscapes of human connection, where each aroma invites exploration, understanding, and a deepening of bonds.

As the festival night draws to a close, under the night sky and canopy of stars, the townspeople gather on the beach, where land meets sea. At this moment, surrounded by the collective aroma of their community—salt, earth, flowers, and the many scents of home—they realize that these fragrances tie them together, crafting a narrative of belonging and shared destiny.

Poetic Perspective:

In a coastal town where sea and earth embrace,
A mosaic of lives, a dance of grace.
Each soul, each being, with a scent so pure,
Weaves a tale of connection, enduring and sure.

Marina walks, the ocean's daughter,
Her scent a mix of salt and water.
With every step, a story unfolds,
Of marine wonders, vast and bold.

Luca, in gardens of green delight,
Carries the earth's fragrance, day and night.
Soil and rain, his constant friends,
In his aroma, nature blends.

Amira, with her ancient art,
Blends scents that touch the heart.
Each fragrance, a memory, a dream,
In her bottles, life's stories gleam.

Once a year, under the star's soft glow,
The town's festival, a sensory show.
Marina, Luca, Amira's scents entwine,
In a symphony of aromas, divine.

On the beach, as the festival ends,
Amongst the scents, a message sends.
The sea, the earth, the flowers' bloom,
In their fragrance, their stories loom.

This town, this community, bound by scent,
A world of aromas, wonderfully lent.
In this narrative of olfactory ties,
The essence of connection lies.

In the coastal town's embracing arms,
The scents converge, weaving charms.
A reminder, in each breath of air,
Of the invisible threads in life we share.

Reflection

This story is a celebration of scent's invisible yet powerful role in connecting us to the world around us. Through the lives of Marina, Luca, and Amira and the vibrant tapestry of their coastal town, the narrative invites readers to acknowledge and cherish the scents that define our existence—the aroma of beginnings, the fragrance of our journeys, and the traces we leave in the hearts of those we touch.

This blend of individual tales and collective experiences poignantly reminds us of the complex, aromatic web of life that binds us. It urges us to breathe deeply, explore the scents that surround us, and recognize the profound connections they forge in the tapestry of our shared human experience.

The narrative offers a rich, olfactory tapestry that captures the essence of community, interconnectedness, and the human condition through the lens of scent. This story unfolds in a small coastal town, presenting a vivid portrayal of how individual lives, each marked by unique aromas, contribute to the collective story of their community. Here's a detailed exploration of the themes and messages portrayed:

The Power of Scent to Define Identity and Connection

Each character—Marina, Luca, and Amira—carries a unique scent that reflects their passions, professions, and personalities. Marina's oceanic aroma, Luca's earthy essence, and Amira's crafted fragrances serve as olfactory signatures that define their identities and facilitate connections. The narrative underscores how scent can act as an invisible thread, weaving individuals into the fabric of their communities and highlighting its role in forming and fostering relationships.

The Role of Nature and Environment in Shaping Human Experiences

The coastal setting emphasizes the deep bond between humans and their natural environment, suggesting that our surroundings profoundly influence our identities, experiences, and the scents we carry. This theme invites readers to reflect on their relationship with the natural world and consider how the environment shapes their sensory experiences and interactions with others.

Scent as a Carrier of Memories and Emotions

Through the characters' individual stories and the collective experience of the festival, the narrative explores how scents are intricately tied to memories and emotions. The festival's carnival of aromas acts as a sensory journey that evokes shared memories, strengthening the bonds within the community. This theme illustrates scent's unique ability to transport us across time and space, triggering emotional responses and recollections that bind us to our past and each other.

Community and Cultural Heritage

The annual festival serves as a focal point, symbolizing the celebration of the town's cultural heritage and the natural beauty that surrounds it. It showcases how communal traditions and celebrations can foster a sense of belonging and unity, creating a shared identity that transcends individual differences. The narrative suggests that these gatherings, imbued with the collective aromas of the community, are essential in maintaining the town's social fabric.

Interconnectedness and Shared Destiny

Ultimately, the story conveys a message of interconnectedness and shared destiny, illustrating how the individual scents of Marina, Luca, Amira, and others blend into a collective aroma that tells the story of their community. This convergence of scents at the festival, against the backdrop of the sea and stars, symbolizes the unity of human experiences—the idea that, despite our differences, we are all part of a larger narrative woven together by the threads of our shared experiences, emotions, and the scents that define them.

"The Scent of Beginnings" is a compelling invitation to appreciate scent's subtle yet powerful role in our lives. It encourages readers to explore the surrounding aromas and recognize how these scents connect us, our memories, and the world. This narrative celebrates the diversity of human experience while highlighting the universal threads that bind us together in the intricate mosaic of life.

Epilogue: The Harmonic Senses

As we reach the coda of our sensory odyssey, we find ourselves immersed in the symphony of senses that compose the essence of love. Through the stories of touch, taste, sound, vision, and scent, we have explored how love speaks to, binds, and transforms us. Love, in its most profound form, is a rich tapestry of sensory interactions, each thread interwoven with the delicate intricacies of human connection and the deep-seated desire to understand and be understood.

The journey has revealed that touch connects us through the warmth of presence, a silent language that speaks volumes in the gentle brush of fingers or the comforting embrace of a hug. It has shown us how taste can evoke memories and forge new ones, binding us together in the shared rituals of meals and exploring flavors that resonate with our histories and hopes. We have heard how sound shapes our emotional landscapes, from the melody of a loved one's laughter to the harmony of voices joined in understanding, creating a resonance that echoes in the chambers of our hearts.

Vision has unfolded before us as a gateway to profound seeing, beyond mere looking, to perceiving the soulful beauty in another's essence and the shared visions that guide our paths forward. And scent has woven its invisible magic, reminding us that the nature of connection often lies in the subtleties and aromas that trigger memories, evoke emotions, and draw us inexorably toward each other.

The symphony of the senses celebrates the myriad ways love makes sense through the senses, urging us to cultivate a deeper, more holistic approach to love. It invites us to savor each note, listen intently to the harmonies and dissonances that define our relationships, and embrace the sensory experiences that enrich our connections. This symphony encourages us to explore the spaces between the notes, the silences, and the subtleties that are as integral to the music of love as the sounds themselves.

In this reflective conclusion, we are reminded that to love and be loved is to engage fully with the world and each other, and to open ourselves to life's full spectrum of sensory experiences. It is a call to listen with our hearts, see with our souls, touch with intention, taste with passion, and inhale the essence of our shared humanity.

As we turn the final page of this sensory exploration, let us carry forward the lessons learned, the connections deepened, and the love discovered on this journey. May we continue to weave the symphony of senses into the fabric of our lives, celebrating love in all its sensory dimensions and embracing the beautiful, complex tapestry it creates.

Appendices: Engaging the Senses

In this section, we present a collection of practical guides and exercises aimed at helping readers explore and enrich their sensory experiences of love. These tools deepen connections in tangible, experiential ways, inviting you to engage each sense with mindfulness and creativity. Whether shared with a partner or practiced individually, these activities can open new avenues for connection and understanding.

Touch: The Language of Comfort and Connection

Exercise: Blindfolded Trust Walk

Partners take turns blindfolding each other and guiding the blindfolded partner around a safe space, using only gentle touches and verbal cues. This exercise heightens trust and tactile awareness.

Practice: The Art of Mindful Hugging

Share a hug in which you focus on the sensation of the embrace, counting slowly to ten together. This practice promotes a broader sense of physical connection and presence.

Taste: Exploring Flavors of Affection

Activity: Mystery Taste Test

Prepare small, bite-sized portions of familiar and new foods. Blindfold your partner and feed them each item, asking them to guess and describe the flavors. This playful activity encourages exploration and communication.

Guide: Creating a Memory Meal

Choose a significant meal for your relationship or create a new dish that combines elements from each person's favorite foods. Focus on the preparation and savoring process as a shared journey.

Sound: Harmonizing Hearts

Exercise: Shared Silence

Spend silence together, sitting comfortably close. Use this time to attune to each other's presence and the ambient sounds. This practice fosters nonverbal communication and mutual appreciation.

Activity: Personal Soundtrack

Create a playlist of songs that are meaningful to your relationship or evoke particular emotions you've shared. Listen together, discussing the memories or feelings each song brings up.

Vision: Seeing Through the Heart's Eye

Practice: Eye Gazing

Sit facing each other and engage in eye gazing for a few minutes, attempting to communicate love and appreciation without words. This intense exercise can foster emotional intimacy and connection.

Activity: Memory Capturing

Take turns photographing each other in places with special meaning to your relationship. Focus on capturing the essence of the moment and the emotions it emits, then share and discuss your perspectives.

Scent: The Essence of Memory and Desire

Exercise: Scent Memory Sharing

People select an object or fragrance that gives off a strong memory or emotion. They share these, describing the memories and feelings associated with each scent.

Guide: Creating a Shared Scent

Mix essential oils or natural scents to create a unique fragrance that represents your relationship. Discuss the emotions and memories you hope this scent will provide.

These exercises and practices are starting points for deeper exploration and engagement with the sensory dimensions of love. By mindfully engaging each sense, you can discover new depths to your connections, enriching your relationships in profound and lasting ways.